WOMEN IN DISGUISE

WOMEN IN DISGUISE

Stories by Marjorie Agosín

Translated by
Diane Russell-Pineda

Azul Editions
MCMXCVI

Published by *Azul Editions*
7804 Sycamore Drive
Falls Church, VA 22042

Grateful acknowledgment is made to
Wellesley College for their support of
the translation of these stories.

ISBN 0-885214-01-4
Library of Congress Catalog Number: 95-75220

Printed in the United States of America

First Edition
10 9 8 7 6 5 4 3 2 1

CONTENTS

WANDERERS, CHAPTER III

DEATH SOUNDS, CHAPTER IV

TICKLE OF LOVE, CHAPTER V

BOUGAINVILLAEA INSOMNIA, CHAPTER VI

THE COLORS OF SILENCE

Marjorie Agosín has entrusted me to give voice to her words in English. In so doing, the present translation of *Women in Disguise*, was to become an endeavor which involved the contour of many voices. While the author has courageously given voice to those who are not heard, or have been forced to silence, the translator was asked to explore the energy and tenor of those voices under the guise of a different culture. At the same time, the voices expressed in these stories are a written vocalization of the lives of women who have often experienced outrageous misfortune and yet do not lose their sense of humor or humanity. Above all, they never lose their sense of direction. These are also common, remarkable voices capable of soaring to heightened states of imagination and physical awareness in climates which are at once the entanglement of recovered memory, horrific and sublime dreams, the crude reality of body mutilation, and simple acts of love. Many of the women who inhabit these pages have been left holding monstrous question marks in their arms, because their loved ones vanished one day, and not even their graves can be located. As a result, they have become filled with inner voices which ask searing questions and keep a solemn vow to recreate the ashes of stolen memory.

The reconstruction of memory in these spoken voices of *Women in Disguise* engages a journey of the senses and a refined complexity of expression. Resonance and tonality of voice mingle with the overpowering memory of sight and smell. Some of the characters are able to permeate borderlands between life and death much the same way certain odors seeped through the walls of enormous gas chambers. Contours of light through sealed doors give notice of a pervading spirit whose life has been unaccounted for. The sky breaks into the narrator's thought; it is both sinister and beautiful, it is ocean and prison. This is a geography of visual textures and aromas placed within a delicate music of words. Colors also have profound and unusual dimensions. And it is in this universe of senses that the author presents us with her lavishly woven poetic hand. Water and light, green hues and radiant transparencies, the fragrance of an old beach house, or the odor of open wounds recall contradictory states of mind which dwell in life, in a simple caress, or the presumed deaths of the tortured and the disappeared. Needless to say, the translator enters these perplexing realms and attempts to endow them with another coloration of the tongue.

While grounded in the reality of the recent dictatorship in Chile, some of the women who speak within the texture of these stories are also faced with more mundane conflicts, which speak for example, to old age, bothersome relatives, their husbands and lovers, and the simple differences between what society has fated for them and their own desires. But it is important to note that all of the women are determined to understand themselves and ask questions of the world. For instance, there is a young Jewish girl who confronts a Catholic priest and women who wish to divest themselves of lonely marriages. One child happily speaks to the dead, while another woman deals with life in a convent, although she herself is not a nun. Yet another woman is a dreamer who is only able to conjure up memory when she is naked. Silence also takes on many colors for each of these women. It is torture and contentment, finality and meditation, physical love and sheer loneliness, or the portentous lure of fear and grief.

These are oral stories, all the better to be read out loud. They are brimming with the crux of human existence and written with sometimes unimaginable combinations of words; bursts of fury and tenderness. And so, the writer and the translator search the breath of the word, looking inside of it like a sacred glass object. Each one will approach with different tints and hues. Each one will ask the voices to speak in order to release the colors of silence.

— Diane Russell-Pineda

FOREWORD

"Curriculum Vitae," one of two poems included in *Women in Disguise* and the first text in the collection, is important for at least two reasons. On the one hand, it focuses on the author's identity, which is at the center of much of Marjorie Agosín's writing, and on the other, it offers important information about the literary tradition within which she writes.

A second generation Chilean Jew, Agosín was born in the United States, lived her first fourteen years in Chile, and has since resided in this country. Unlike most Hispanic writers in the U.S., however, Agosín writes in Spanish, and considers herself a Spanish American, not a Latina writer ("Publications: *I don't go North / Only South*"). Her literary production is firmly anchored in the Spanish American literary tradition about which she has written extensively in some of the most important Spanish American and U.S. publications in the field. Although her work in the United States has frequently been connected to that of Latinas, her literary models are Spanish American women writers such as Gabriel Mistral, María Luisa Bombal (Chile). Silvina Ocampo (Argentina). Margo Glantz and Rosario Castellanos (Mexico).

Her contributions to Spanish American culture are not only in the literary arena. From the mid-seventies to the mid-eighties, Agosín was deeply committed to human rights and a vocal defender of the victims of the Southern Cone military dictatorships. Her books on the Mothers of the Plaza de Mayo (*Mothers of the Plaza*), and on the "arpilleristas" (*Scraps of Life*), contributed to the denouncement of human rights violations against women in Argentina and Chile. Her sensitivity to these issues, however, has not been limited to this geographical area; Agosín has also denounced human rights abuses in Central America and she has devoted part of her work to the collection of women's testimonies. In Spanish America women, especially those who do not belong to the governing elites, have limited access to public discourse. How women have circumvented the limitations of verbal discourse placed upon them is a topic which Agosín has explored both in her critical and her creative writing. The topic recurs in *Women in Disguise*. When Violeta, the character of "Bonfires," is feeling both marginalized and threatened by verbal discourse, she burns the books in her house and begins to rewrite the stories by cutting up clothing "and that is how the stories came out of her hands."

One of Agosín's concerns in her previous work, which is also present in several stories in *Women in Disguise* is how to (re)construct a past which should have kept her in Spanish America but which displaced her instead. This is the main objective of *A Cross and a Star*, which recounts the experience of the Jewish girl Frida Halpern, Agosín's mother, during her adolescence in Osorno. There were only two Jewish families in this southern Chilean city among a large population of Germans who favored the policies of the Third Reich. Frida begins her story as she turns 13, close to the age Agosín was when leaving Chile. In telling her mother's memories Agosín recovers, albeit vicariously, a past which Agosín never fulfilled and about which she can never stop wondering and dreaming. Memory is also related in her work to her Jewish identity. As "Last Names," the second text in *Women in Disguise* exemplifies, the construction of her genealogy and the establishment of connections with her ancestors, many of whom died in Nazi concentration camps, are central to her definition as an individual and as a Jewish writer. Most of Marjorie's work, in fact, is driven by her need to establish links with both her Jewish and her Spanish American identities. Her Jewish grandparents who emigrated to Chile from both Austria and Russia, are recurrent characters in her stories ("The Messiah," "Olga").

Women in Disguise is a version of *Las alfareras* (1994; *Women Potters*). The English version differs considerably from the original in that the author has both added and excised texts and recognized the material. Although each version is essentially a different book, in both renditions *Women in Disguise* is a collection of fragments, poetic prose, and short stories which develop various thematic concerns. The overriding objective of the book is to represent the basic ambiguity of individual experience and to expand the boundaries of perception. The texts collected in *Women in Disguise* present worlds which are seemingly simply but in fact are multilayered constructions where the oneiric, the fantastic, and the magical coexist with the ordinary and material representations of time and space. The characters, who often dissolve in their precarious discursive existence, inhabit fluid realms where the boundaries between the material and the ideal, the conscious and the unconscious, the human and the natural tend to disappear. Chance becomes in several instances the medium enabling these characters to go beyond the looking glass: "She prefers incongruence and the drowsy extravagance of disorderly things. She likes to explore the rhythm of invisible animals . . . Each morning she takes a walk in no particular direction almost touching the depths of the trees." ("The Wanderer")

Many of these texts belong, of course, to the Spanish American literary tradition of magic realism, which, according to the Cuban writer Alejo Carpentier, one of its founders and theorists, proposes that in Spanish America the magical and the real are part and parcel of everyday life, that they are integral elements of the Spanish American world. In reading these texts, however, especially the short stories many of which favor the creation of an atmosphere over the development of a plot, one is also reminded of the dreamlike and fantastic worlds of Remedios Varo, the Spanish painter who produced her most important work in the mid 50s and early 60s while living in Mexico. The congruence of Agosín's and Varo's work, whom Agosín admires and whose work she knows well, include the female figure as the prime connecter, discoverer and inhabitant of the magical and fantastic dimensions of reality. As in Varo, Agosín's female characters venture deeply into the natural world, especially watery landscapes, rivers, and the sea, but also the forest shrouded in mist, in search of a freedom which society generally denies them. As in Varo, who frequently painted figures which bear unmistakable resemblance to herself, many of Agosín's stories are firmly anchored in her own biography. The mixture of the real and the fictional, the transformation of the real into fiction and the fictional into the real become a means of exploring the interstices of reality, that metaphysical dimension which is never too far from the experience of Agosín's characters.

— *Patricia Rubio*

WOMEN IN DISGUISE

WOMEN POTTERS
CHAPTER I

CURRICULUM VITAE

Rebel. Obsessed with missives, love letters
and honey candy.
Publications: *I Don t go North,*
Only South.
How Not to Become Civilized
oregano and semiotics
Hobbies:
fornicator
insomniac
wanderer
gossiper
over-eater
References:
prison
Nelson Mandela
Miguel de Cervantes Saavedra
my mother
Successes:
Random days gazing at the light in southern France
uprooted frenzied nights, intoxicating nights of crazy,
crazy love
My children, Sonia and Joseph.
Sunflowers, tatoos on my skin.

LAST NAMES

It s not my fault my family didn t own any vineyards. That s why I have a scarcity of last names with a taste of champagne or ones which allude to the pleasures of the palate. My family was different. The wealthiest ones set up shop beneath an umbrella in Odessa, and sold second-hand clothes. They called themselves proprietors. The other relatives went into business with the mafia. Although it may seem strange to you, the Sicilians weren't the only ones to gain control of the mafia. The Jews are also involved in this profession, as were my uncles from the other side of the Black Sea.

My relatives are roving gypsies, illiterate, and toothless. They have only one possible profession; tailoring, but not out of laziness or lack of intelligence, (we had plenty of that). You must be aware that Jews were given occupations in the fabric trade because they were banned from attending universities.

In Russia, when my relatives from underneath those umbrellas were hunted down, they departed for Turkey. When they kicked them out of Istanbul, they continued on to Marseille, where my father was born, who also was kicked out of the hospital because he was a Jew. They finally landed on the Pacific coast, where Jews were not exactly loved. They were just ignored. Now of course, you must understand about last names. I am seated across from you. I am wearing patent leather shoes, white stockings, and a small white hat, made in Taiwan. I live in Paris. And you inquire about the origin of my last name, which doesn t sound familiar to you because I don t belong to one of the four or five fashionable Chilean families. I am not a Balmaceda, an Irarrázabal, or an Aldunate. Oh, but of course, there is Señorita Pía . . . My name has been changed so many times, except that Agosín, is not a French name, and before that, it was something else. Isn t that the way it goes?

Quite boldly, I tell her: Señorita, I am Jewish. That means I am lacking a pedigree. I have horns. I am an extortionist and a mafiosi. You blush and tell me you are sorry. Sorry? Why? Is it because I belong to the most chosen and most persecuted people on earth?

Señorita, don t blush. I am not ashamed that I don t have the 'right' last name, or social status, or the opportunity to become an ambassador. These little horns don t make me feel ashamed either. Among my people there are poets, mathematicians, psychologists, painters, and Talmud scholars who scratch their noses and study what the Talmud says about nose scratching. I am a relative of Freud, Marx, Marc Chagall, and maybe the Balmaceda family. . .

Naturally, you don t know my family. They don t own newspaper chains or real estate. Some of them have candy stores, others have fur factories. Most of them are doctors. And I write poems that I retail for a dollar.

Señorita, thank you for your question. I don t know whether I am Chilean, gringa, or Bostonian. Countries and flags get tangled up on me. But I am sure of one thing: I don t eat ham on Friday, and I fast once a year, not out of religious duty, but more out of respect for my relatives who set up shop beneath that umbrella, and also to honor the memory of my grandfather Joseph, who used to say that God is everywhere, even in a head of lettuce.

That is what I am Señorita, the essence of a history that goes back thousands of years. I am not a Errázuriz or a Subercaseaux. I ll never have a political post or hear them say behind my back; How about that shitty Jew working for the government? That is my story, Señorita. You and I look alike. We are both blond and wear little elastic stockings. All you need is the hat. Both of us are women. You with your extra-long last name, with lots of *r*'s in it, and your fine pedigree. I have a short last name, one which is unpredictable. I come from profiteers, merchants, and candy store owners. When it is all said and done, I am well aware of who I am. To you, I am a shitty Jew. To my grandfather I am a Russian princess whose arms were never branded, someone they let live.

SILENCES

I

Silence chose me. My words grew thin, and suddenly my voice became a fading sound within the roundness of my throat. Silence held me between its walls of green shadow, and I too was happy. I stopped talking. I wrote long love letters delivered by my messengers who were always waiting to find out if I would ever again emit the tweet of some passionate bird. But I have been mute for twenty years, alone with the glorious silence of gestures, alone with the stories I read and read again. Alone with words that are only written and sacred, words that are never spoken out loud or on the high seas of sound.

II

Often, I dream about my voice. It is the voice that is still inside me, unsettled and moveable, like what is found in the inner space of water. And then it vanishes.

III

On the streets of the city they shout: "There goes the little woman who can't talk," and others say, "The Jew." I am glad I am not able to respond. I still have a skirt the color of water and my green sandals from every forest and insomnia.

IV

Sometimes I look at my hands and find miraculous cracks

inside of them. I remember certain words like waves that move in the clearest and deepest silence. Words are like fragrances and the ocean, and I wrap myself in their immensity. Then I am no longer sick. In the province of speech, I am a firefly.

Memory's echo on the tip of the tongue. To say what one might want to say. They come to visit me and I bow invisibly to them. Nonetheless, they call me the poor mute. And I write to them on that gigantic wall to tell them that silence has chosen me.

V

One day, in a year of intrepid seasons, wordlessly, I love you and place my tongue to rest upon yours.

VI

Within silence there are certain sounds which have louder tones. Like the steps of the dead when they enter a bright dining room, or my sisters preparing for the inertia of the evening, or me, inside my universe of constellations and silences. I accompany them as if on a lethargic journey.

VII

When I lost my voice, he clasped my hands. He warmed the lamps and all the gestures of love, and made words inside my mouth.

For a long time I was close to the silence of the garden.

I was cold in the dark shadows and terrified of the cypress trees. But I rested there in the quiet of that forest, so piercing, so evil and so beautiful.

Now I am told that perhaps I will be able to speak. And I am delighted to invent the softness of syllables. I repeat the alphabet and imagine a chain of verbs. It is delicious to know that I will be able to cry out to you and tell you I love you.

I attend sumptuous parties with a mask on. It is a glittering mask like the ones that are worn at the Carnival of Venice. No one knows I cannot talk even though my tongue is tied to my heart. Everyone discusses business trips and maids. The men become aroused with the possible idea of making love to a woman who is mute.

I sit at the head of a great banquet. I am next to a businessman, the owner of slaves and mangos. My mother is growing bored next to me, and fans herself with Egyptian parchments. I am growing old next to so many words.

CONVENTS

No one knows how the woman with the effervescent red shoes and silk stockings arrived at the convent. No one knows how she appeared beneath the walls of that city without a sea where decapitated swallows meander about, where all of darkness is a thirsty and invading hand. But she is there, watched over by the tiny nuns in her ocher colored coffin cell filled with stars. She insists that the windows be opened to release that old smell, that urine smell which clings to the skin like the wounds of women who have lost their memory.

At night she undresses and prays to a cross of pink wood. And she is the one who made fun of the Lord's prayer all of her life. She is the one who preferred this earthly paradise, her perspiring legs, and a secret kiss on her pubis. There she is, as if in pain and half-asleep. The nuns do not allow her to open the windows because she is unable to touch the heavens and the tips of her fingers are injured. With her gaze of dry trees and shaken dreams she cannot be happy.

She has been in that cell for so long now that she gets the cadences of time all mixed up. She believes that at last she has touched those final depths and is familiar with peace. Sometimes she is joyful when she opens the small balustrade and peeks out at the reddish bougainvillaea flowers in the austere landscape of that large house inhabited by whispers. That is when she dreams, inventing horses, purplish-red scorpions, the bodies of pastures, a mouth making love to her, holding on to her, creating memory from a landscape.

No one knows how she came to the convent with her loneliness branded on her, with her red shoes and gashed stockings, dragging with her the odor of urine and exile like an open window.

STRIP TEASE

Although it may seem complicated, undressing in front of a stranger is a fast and simple process. One might even say it is natural, especially when a man and a woman desire each other with frantic clumsiness. One look, and words about God uttered in low tones, are all that is needed for pieces of clothing and pathetic objects covering the body to explode onto the emptiness of the floor.

OLGA/OLGA

We liked to go to the village when the tide was golden like chalices of maize. Every summer in the afternoon we used to walk down narrow streets with half-empty hotels and a few old women fanning themselves, consumed by a time of memory. We liked to visit Olga's store. It was on a corner and faced the bay. Olga wore black clothing and tight blouses. Her breasts looked like snowy milk spilling down her pale body, fluttering and restless.

Olga was an herbalist and a student of butterflies. She had an endless number of miracle plants for love sickness and forests of lavender stored in tiny glass jars. She had come from the Baltic Sea and had amber eyes and hair the color of corn. She swore to be a fortuneteller, but clients were scarce. No one told her secrets or gave her any gifts. Olga looked like one more object stuck in that corner store facing the sea where she hoarded newspapers gone foul by the passage of time, and things that happiness never got to know.

For a long time I visited Olga knowing that she too was an impostor. I pretended to be from another country and she pretended to tell fortunes. But the truth was that we were just two solitary beings, weary from so many ocean voyages and so many journeys by train.

Olga used to cover up her arms just like I did. She says it's because her tattoo is very enticing, but only I know the truth. In reality, she wears a tattoo from Auschwitz on her arm and covers it with the feathers of a dove and black laces. I too was in Auschwitz, and in order to invent memory, I used to imagine long concerts with violins and flutes, and sometimes I told the other women prisoners I was descended from gypsies and that in my dreams I was able to foretell who would live and who would die.

Olga doesn't know I saw her with her head shaved, blindly walking in her sleep through forests of wires and unmentionable fields. She doesn't know that I saw her agitated, skeletal body up close. And now, she is pretty with milky breasts that lean out so people will notice as she passes by. Like the rest of us, Olga keeps her hands covered and hidden.

Olga has a husband named Vladimir. He didn't go to Auschwitz, but he never tells which hell he was in. He only has one hand. On the other arm he has a violet colored hook that is also supposed to be able to fathom dreams and predict the future by only giving it a touch. When Vladimir gets close to Olga with his violet glove, his hook, like a pirate captain of long ago, she desires his caresses and lets herself be touched by a man whose hands watch over his stories like plants that only grow between the shadows.

Olga and I have become friends. I help her collect words that only grow in the light. I help her dry the lavender of tranquility. And yesterday was the first time she invited me to her house. Olga lives on a hill surrounded by breezes and the sea. She collects skeletons and scattered bones and says they are the bones of memory. She also has two enormous bathtubs and in the evening, when the wind appears like a galloping, one-armed witch, when the frightened stars have hidden themselves with the sunflowers of the day, Olga takes off all her clothes and sits down to imagine the burden of the night and the fragility of each day — there inside her bathtub by the light of a thousand invisible stars.

I also went with her to meet the shadow of the night. We undressed so we could see each other's arms. We had the same amber eyes. We didn't know which shower, or in which garden of devils our parents had remained. We didn't know whether to talk or remain silent, whether to predict the future of others or our own, whether to play guessing games or beads. There was always the possibility of inventing ourselves, of denying that it was possible that they had branded our hands, shaved our heads, slapped us until we entered a sea of shadows.

Olga and I looked at the moonless sky, the skeletons all around us reassuring us that death would continue. It is the first time I saw her naked, and we are wearing the same number, this tattoo from an unmentionable memory.

LETTERS

By vocation I am an epistolary sleepwalker. I have been writing letters in this pink and blue cellar now for fifty five years. When daybreak appears like a sleepless canvas, I rise. I like the cellar because it is quiet and deep. I write in this trustworthy place, away from rage, but close to love. It is my task to compose words with precise cadences and rhythms. I write letters for the sake of happiness, and to protect grief and honor. Each morning, I surrender the entire workday to writing clairvoyant letters. What I mean to say is that I write to those imaginary beings who appear to me at about three o clock in the afternoon, the hour when the cellar levitates from tranquility. That time is for them, especially for two or three of my imaginary lovers, to whom I dedicate hours of mischievous and infuriating missives. I talk to them about desire and the color of lips right after love making. Often, I arrive in silence, and allow them to see the everlasting blood, that excruciating blood, like the gestures of bleeding women.

In the afternoon, I devote endless hours to fugitives or criminals, to those who killed out of love or hunger. There are twenty six prisoners who receive my words daily. My letters are a tremendous consolation for wounds in the soul, spasms, or curing fear in people who stutter. I know the prisoners are very pleased with my words. For example, I tell them things like this: Today is December, 31, 1938. In Europe, war and forests of wire are being talked about. But from my window, I can see a blue glass, the sun, a sunset, and the memory of rocks and the sea.

When dusk comes, tiny rats surround me. They like to be near me, and I also feel them close when they slide around inside my mouth. They are so clandestine and short tempered as they run wild through the percale. It is at that moment, when my dream looks like a knife clouded by time, that I begin to ponder about who I will write to. I think perhaps it is time to correspond with the dead, with those who departed this kingdom without any message or explanatory statement. Then I go to the obituary section of the newspaper to see who died. Now, don t think that I write to their soulful relatives. My letters go addressed to the general cemetery. I tell the deceased certain things, like the fact that the earth has a protective layer of dust. I tell them they are not alone, and that the world is a secluded, subterranean gardenia.

I never leave the cellar because confinement and letters are my calling, even though they have been lying there in a pile like a smoky bonfire for the last fifty five years. No one comes to pick them up. They tremble along with the movements and occupations of the seasons. They look like the blankets of autumn, but they are still there there. I am happy thinking about them, thinking that tomorrow I ll write about so many things. And I will begin with these words: I am Eduviges Siverman. I live in a cellar. I have been writing letters for years. I like watercolor paints. I don t like to talk about diseases. I only write love letters.

BONFIRES

No one thought it out of the ordinary to look up at the sky, almost high enough to break a neck, and see the extravagant clouds of smoke arising from Violeta Acevedo s narrow and nearly wretched patio. Her neighbors had labeled her a weird old woman because she had the custom of feeding maimed cats and filling her house with small, oarless, land boats. And the day the military came, when she shaved her head and began the daily burning of books, the neighbors did not become upset.

The first books to be burned were the ones with gray, red, and blue covers. Then came the ones with a few short lines written in them, and some people believed that those must have been books of poetry. The essence of the words Violeta systematically burned was of no consequence, because she said that the day they knocked at her door, as they had done in Varsovia, they would find her with the Talmud in her hands.

No one came to her door. The smoke clouds grew smaller and almost invisible. But on that patio, it was always possible to find a quiet rubble of pain, and Violeta, all shrunken up, holding a demented and churlish silk handkerchief, contemplating the sky and the enormous menacing clouds which foretold the thunderous arrival of the military. And so, on a day she least imagined, like evil or good omens, they appeared at her door. They saw the empty bookshelves and proceeded to the next room where they took away the deaf mute who was always on a journey, demolished within the silence of misfortune.

The next day the tiny smoke clouds were gone and the sky near Violeta s patio returned with the same magnificent tranquility as the hollyhocks and pink roses. On a mahogany table, Violeta began to cut up clothing. She cut up the deaf man s clothes; his pants, his undershirts, and undershorts, which had the appearance of sleepless shrouds. And that is how the stories came out of her hands.

GUILLERMINA AGUILAR

As if out of a dream, Guillermina Aguilar was born from the very roots of the floor of the earth. She is porous and leans forward. Guillermina Aguilar doesn t know the alphabet. But I am certain that letters, one blue sound, and time itself grow out of her hands. From before her birth she was a potter, as was her mother, and her mother s mother. Guillermina came to understand the secrets of slick black clay, water and soil.

Through her hands flow paintings, translucent everyday objects, spoons, clay vessels, women pausing at the market, death strolling about with a basket of maguey, fruit syrup, and sweet basil.

Throughout the evening and for days on end, Guillermina toils without respite because she owns the hands of a bird. I draw near her to bathe in the rhythm of the clay. She tells me she likes to make vessels so she can put gardenias inside of them. She says that knowing how to read doesn t matter because the words flow out of her hands.

THE CEMETERY

for Diane Russell-Pineda

The little girl lived in the cemetery because her grandmother, who possessed an ancestral devotion for taking care of the dead and keeping their graves watered and groomed, had been born there. She lived near the oldest graves, in the part of the cemetery where more flowers grew and the moss was like a dense jungle or a lagoon of shining green colors. This was where dwelled, in among the flower filled graves, with a hen and a squirrel.

In the evening when the wind made gigantic tattoos across the flatlands and the world sought refuge to ward off its grief, the little girl would talk to the dead. She spoke very slowly so they wouldn t awaken from their magnificent sleep, and often, in a low voice, she would tell them some of her secrets. And then, as if the tombs themselves were bewitching lamps that glowed with the breath of a human voice, she would rub them once again.

The little girl grew up in the cemetery. And even though she had contact with the world of the living, that was the place she wanted to be. She went to school during the day, learning the names of some of the trees and how to spell. But daylight learning and the repetition of ravishing syllables and vowels didn t interest her. She liked returning to the cemetery because there, the texture of the birds, their tails of gleaming layers, and the breath of the wind, were all unmistakably clear. She liked to follow certain paths and visit the ones who had been dead for more than a century. She felt safe with them because right in the middle of a bird s song they were completely silent. She liked to hug their gravestones and imagine that soon the ghosts would come out to clap for her when they saw her pass by.

The little girl grew old along with the cemetery. And when it was time for her to die, she settled herself into her favorite place, and dressed herself in orchids, hollyhocks, lilies, and violets. At last, she would be one of them. But when she died, no one went to visit the dead anymore. No one cleaned off their gravestones or kept the weeds cut. The cemetery and its cities fell into the most forgotten of forgotten states.

ALFAMA[1]

She likes to wait for that tenuous hour when desire subtly disturbs her like an unexpected silence. She likes the darkness when animals search for a place to take cover. She is preparing herself for the nocturnal season. The night is a wild feast of sacred parks. Her body, a transgression of love. On her skin she wears tattoos; orchids and other flowers. There are gardenias on her ears, and her thighs — kindled in the roundness of her pubis staring at her wide-open as if she were an accomplice to the origins of darkness and the turmoil of the evening.

She climbs the stairs of that stony passage, that shanty town of the city where the Phoenicians, troubled by the copper flow of the sea, took shelter in the evenings so they could hear the gentle breath of the shore and throb impatiently like the clock of flowers inside their salty mouths. She climbs and they look on her. Some of them applaud as they watch her pass by. They already know who she is. A few of them follow her on horseback, others follow her on the sly, snatching away the happiness she carries between her legs. Danger exerts an intoxicating power over her making her fall and go around in circles until she touches the depths of time and those of her own body. She does not remove her clothes until she arrives at the citadels where those navigators who have no boats are waiting for her, as are the beggars who also know how to savor her. She approaches them only to return their glances but not as an offering or a token of love. And she lets them kiss her and have her because they are the owners of Alfama who now draw close to her, foul-mouthed and without disguise, to feel the tender breath of gardenias and the ocean seaweed wind that she keeps at the end of her ears. She likes to feel that drop of sweat choking her, the breath of the beggars, the transvestites, and history falling from her hair, because danger is eternally sweet. Because at last, the savage heart of the evening has come.

[1]Ancient Moorish sector of Lisbon, Portugal.

RITUALS
CHAPTER II

FIRST COMMUNION

All of my neighborhood friends were preparing to make their first communion. They didn t need to study a lot or even buy reading glasses. All they had to do was collect colorful religious cards and look for the finest lace for their organdy outfits. As Jewish girls, we didn t have religious cards or little angels with gigantic wings. No one prayed for us at bedtime and we didn t know how to go about saying prayers either. But we did believe in those invisible angels who were always in mourning.

It was strange to be a Jewish girl with a tiny star of David concealed around my slender neck that shook whenever someone called out to us, There go the Jew dogs who ate up the bread from the oven. We didn t have pink lace dresses or small virgins made out of wax to decorate the garden. Everything was hushed like a vague and subtle silence.

My mother was not fond of prayer because she said that the unmentionable one was everywhere. But I couldn t see him. And at the very least, I wanted to be able to keep him in my pocket the way my friends kept their religious cards or the things they cherished.

My friend Emma promised to take me to confession before she made her first communion, and she told me I d have to pretend to be a Christian girl. I remember it was a foggy winter in Santiago with soft rains making way for spring. I covered my head with a blue wool cap and wore one of my sister s trailing skirts. Together,

Emma and I headed for the church downtown. At the corner, thin, inebriated women were selling candles and votive offerings.

When we arrived, Emma made me go toward a small door enclosed in darkness. It was a hideous little dwelling, and next to it was a skinny, naked man supporting his hands and body on a blue cross. The music made my hair stand on end, and the smell of ashes made me believe I had arrived upon the threshold of death or those wicked blue gas chambers my mother was always cursing.

Emma signaled for me to kneel down and lean toward a badly frayed, foul-smelling curtain. A man with a bird-like voice whispered to me, Daughter, do you touch your body? I told him that I did, that I always touched it, everyday. I touched it when I cleaned my teeth, scrubbed my hands, or brushed my hair, and that sometimes, I touched my breasts, which were growing like sunflowers underneath the covers.

Daughter, do you touch yourself everyday?

Yes, I said, proud of the truth.

Tell me your sins, he said, half cursing, half seducing me.

Not one, Mr. Father priest, not one sin. I can t remember my sins, I am a Jewish girl, I said.

Warily, I rose, untangling myself from those shaggy, dark curtains. I went home and forgot to brush my teeth and comb my hair.

I like to hear my mother praying in silence. I became used to the fact that there were no angels with huge wings to watch over my sleep — only the immense solitude of the evening, a blanket of stars, and the wild heart that dreams have.

WOMEN IN DISGUISE

My mother and her friends were fond of talking about the maids. And sometimes, with a tone that suggested a perfect mixture of the irony and respect of these false ladies, they used to call them 'household advisors. Late afternoons, facing a conceited mirror, I watched them getting ready. Before they straightened out their shiny stockings, they put make up on their legs which were covered with deep, green varicose veins. But to me, they looked like the rivers of a wasted adulthood. Then they undid their hair so they would look taller and thinner. But I was sure that in among those irascible locks, they could have kept all of the bird s nests my sister and I collected while the maids kept their distance and their reserve on those huge blue brick patios.

My mother used to tell us she would be back before dark because she had to attend a very stuck-up tea. And for us, it was odd that the women went for tea each week in order to discuss the latest serial novels from Paris, and of course, the maids. At times, when the tea was held at our house, I could hear them saying that the maids were dirty and kept men and flattened geraniums in the back rooms. I also heard them say that they hid children in the sky lights. But the ladies admitted they couldn t live without them. Who was going to wake them up sometime after ten o clock in the morning with a cup of coffee or a wonderful slice of toast with butter? Who would wash their blood stained panties? Nevertheless, the maids were a presence just like the queens of enchanted houses. They would go about like movable furniture and were often conspicuous and pristine like the transparency of a looking glass. I liked them because that kind of humility was not something which was learned. And for me, there was nothing about them that was vain or excessive like my mother s friends who always closed their legs, winked their eyes, and gave off a smell of ingratitude.

My sister and I liked to be with the maids. We were fond of disobeying our elders so we could take refuge in those rooms that seemed like lessons for the body. Those rooms, similar to darkness and something that gets in the way. But we went to visit them to look at photographs of decent little girls, photographs of certain weddings and first communions when they had to ask the lady of the house to borrow a coat. One of them even asked to borrow a stole made from a few of those fateful foxes.

The maids rooms had an aroma of oregano and sausage which hung from the ceiling. A radio kept telling the story of Esmeralda de los Ríos, who fell in love with a man with whom she had a son, and then returned him to the sea.

The maids loved us and kept us protected from curses and the evil eye. So we couldn t imagine that they killed the babies from their eternally round bellies and grease stained aprons.

We liked to sit with the maids on the sidewalk in those armless straw chairs to observe the day s happenings; crazy men picking up cigarette butts, or just the earth falling open at the height of the earthquake season. But we had the most fun with them on those late afternoons when my mother went for tea and the maids dressed up in her clothing; those shiny stockings, brassieres from Paris, and red silk underpants. Then they would look at themselves in the mirror and scream. Startled, by so much joy.

COUSINS

We were cousins when we got married. But you had that gentle, standoffish way of funny cousins who have known each other since a childhood now buried in gossamer outfits and ties which were prudently small. We met in southern Chile, at one of those four o clock parties where people from discreet, noble, families talk to each other along with that insipid cup of tea, (a frustrated memory from our British ancestors).

Conversations flow in two voices. The men wearing ties whose feet are half-asleep like the afternoon, discuss the high price of food and coffee. They talk as if they were the ones who shop at the supermarket, or for that matter, the ones who prepare that magical, sparkling brew which takes them out of their shapeless, flaccid, state.

As reticent women, we spent time talking about having babies, pains in the lower abdomen, our aunt s operation, and without fail, those golden complexions of our British ancestors. That is how we met, in one of those houses in the provinces, in a world like the cloudy edges of a face that only contemplates the park, the plaza, or the stone houses, but never the corn that grows on the American continent.

We talked and looked at each other with that typical confidence of strangers who are able to intuit their alliances. And so, we were married. Our lives passed like those afternoons in which thoughtful married couples sit and drink their tea in the harmony of scattered events. We used to enjoy sitting in our terribly dark living room where a piano carpeted in brown colors let us imagine, or return, to a glorious and fleeting past. We very rarely spoke to each other with that angelic voice happy couples always use. We very rarely caressed each other, and when we did, it was usually in a closed room where the darkness filtered through like a harsh nightmare, devious and painful.

We lived like that for years, allowing ourselves to become remote from laughter and anger. We were together out of duty and custom, talking to each other in a careful way, accepting the fact that children never came, accepting the uneventful passage of yellow afternoons.

One afternoon when the sun was shining madly, proclaiming the arrival of a magnificent spring, I decided to go into town, leaving behind my purse, gloves, and the few jewels my distant husband had given me. I departed with no particular destination, the way I did when I was a teenager, bewildered by my own scent and my step, half-bold and half-fast, breaking loose through the woods and the vastness of a frontier which was enticing and rich, and did not threaten.

I arrived at the town feeling desperate and happy, to the smell of toasted nuts, the noise of conversations brimming with airy, delicious, love, and the silences of my own house made out of stone. Along the way, I ran into a woman selling gardenias. They were fragrant, shiny, exquisite and oval shaped. I bought a small bouquet from her and held it very close to my breast, the way women do who are in love. Then I decided to buy myself a copper ring that looked like gold. The ring just fit on the pale finger of my hand, and it took on the colors of new, thick, leaves. Overcome with joy I walked, almost ran, through the streets of Osorno with the flowers and the ring. I had married myself. I had a bouquet of gardenias, my hidden body had a fragrance, just like the flowers, and my finger took on an incredible essence. Then I knew that I had gotten married for the first time, and I didn t need to go home for tea or wash the sly, gray collars of his shirts. I had married myself. And I was happy. With my bouquet of gardenias held very close to my breast, and my copper ring, I began to take off my clothes.

THE MESSIAH

When my father leaned forward in the brocade sofa and wrapped himself in blue shawls, when the calm of the great house had penetrated every pore and the fog stood still on the araucaria trees, I knew the hour of prayers had come. And with the faith of innocents and children, both devout and betrayed, I also knew I was waiting for the Messiah.

From the time I reached an early age of awareness, I knew my entire family was waiting for that gigantic and amazing man called the Messiah. At first it was puzzling because it didn't make any sense to me. They always spoke about him somewhere between blushing and enraptured, and the few Jews who lived in the village were also waiting for that same individual. Would he arrive at tea time? Would he come after dinner? I learned, however, that certain things are not to be questioned or mentioned, like the name of God or the Messiah.

I came to realize that the history of the Jews has nothing to do with being a chosen people and everything to do with the patience of those who lived thousands of years ago. My father used to tell me that our calendar has five thousand loves, and on the holy days we beat our chests again and again to be reassured that God the unutterable waits for us and will send us the Messiah.

My father died on the same brocade sofa wrapped in blue shawls, waiting for the Messiah. And I watched my mother cover the mirrors on those days of death in order not to see the face of sorrow. Then she sat among the ashes to wait for the Messiah. No one told me if the Messiah was fat or thin, or if he had all of his teeth. Because in the third world, having a complete set of teeth is truly a sign of prestige.

Now I am an old woman with flat breasts, and some of my teeth are missing. I never understood why we were waiting for someone we didn't even believe was in heaven. We can only be absolutely sure about this life, and waiting is one way to cast aside the face of death's holy palpitation.

My now deaf friends think the Messiah was Jesus with his ungraceful hair and his lavish, bright forehead. At my age, I am tired of waiting for a man. I am content to spend hours collecting fireflies and butterflies, awaiting the arrival of the white horses of death. I am madly in love with sunrises that make no deals with life or death. And now that I wait for no one, everyone has descended on the cloaks of my dreams.

CHEPITA

On drowsy evenings, when the twilight was a heavy canvas, my grandmother would talk to Santa Teresita. She told her about her sorrows, the difficulties of being widowed and poor, the pains in her back, her trick finger, and her bad cataract operation. She would lament in soft tones beyond the wee hours of the morning, until she was awakened with fried eggs and whipped coffee.

For months, Josefina was happy conversing with Santa Teresita de los Andes. She had no need to visit the cemetery, because it wasn't the appropriate place for her. And the dead were everywhere, not just confined to those memorial parks.

My grandmother began to take an interest in Santa Teresita when she found out that the saint was fond of gardenias and that her mother had been a prostitute in the villages that lie in the foothills of the mountain range. But more than believing in her miracles, my grandmother liked her face and her garments of water. And even though Santa Teresita was from the Andes mountains, her gaze was of the sea and of something that comes from pale waters.

Then I too began to collect religious cards of Santa Teresita. But rather than confessing to her, I asked for favors which had nothing to do with matters of money. They were only recipes for love. I told her I wanted someone to love me. I requested that earthquakes cease to occur, that my mother be relieved of her uncompromising itch, and above all, that she put a stop to the rising price of coffee.

One day when I was walking on San Cristobal hill with the maids, I began to feel slightly uneasy. I looked up in the sky and there was Santa Teresita all dressed up in violets, just like the ones my grandmother used to take to her dead son. Behind me horns were honking and I could see an array of lights. Santa Teresita was winking at me and showing off her legs to us.

Ever since then, her presence has captivated me. I told my Aunt Luisa about it, the one who bathes the dead in her Jewish neighborhood. She was horrified at my devotion. But in the strictest secret of silence she confessed to me that she had a little religious card of Santa Teresita underneath her nightstand. She said she prayed to her for her children, both living and dead, and had asked her for a cure for spasms and her bad hip.

For years, my family worshiped Santa Teresita de los Andes and made pilgrimages to her shrines. On these occasions, they hid the star of David, and I put on a tiny blue cross. We like Santa Teresita because she has green eyes, but most of all because she has a good soul. So to hell with religions. We are all pagans and rebels.

BIRTHDAY

My mother and I love each other wildly and adoringly. We like to look at each other the way somnambulists do, brushing our drowsy manes, greeting each other from afar, or within the close proximity of our eyes, like two small lakes. We like to make the same gestures, roam the same paths on deserted coasts or the rose filled portals of certain abandoned houses. Often, we make it our custom to visit the shore like two mute women. We tell each other that we are harvesting the seaweed, those locks of self-murdering women. And as we work, we talk of love and the times we used to play; forest of dark rooms, laughing in between the mist and the fog, like faithful partners in crime.

We used to travel together collecting the things of memory. Sometimes we engaged in the purchase of hats belonging to discreet ladies from forgotten drawing rooms. Other days, when the sun is a raging crimson dome, we take shelter beneath a golden umbrella and dream about vast prairies of black sand, a melodious beach, and a joy that is truly ours.

Yesterday, my mother and I decided to go where to the fortune- teller s house. Both of us have a curiosity for everything that has to do with prophesy. But memory is what captivates us most of all. No dead person shall be forgotten or left without water. Windows of forsaken houses shall be left open. And time itself shall not become a fugitive.

We found the fortuneteller on a road marked for exiled women. She had a tender voice like the stars of nocturnal celebrations. She too was of the night, and with her star-filled hair she slowly caressed our hands. She pressed her finger tips deeply into ours, bestowing us with woodlands and alchemy. She clapped for us because she wanted to reassure us that we possessed an aroma of gardenias and good fortune. Then she told us that she read palms; palms to applaud with, palms to eat with, palms to feel beautiful with - beautiful, in a resounding voice. My mother and I didn t ask her about the fortune s of tomorrow. Instead, we inquired after bizarre or missing things. And since together we form a single hand, and one life line, we asked if she would read my mother s left hand, and my right hand.

She told us stories. She told us miracles and tales. Our bodies rose like cranes of love. We had no desire to know about past or future events. We merely took delight as one hand entangled itself with the other, and then the other, drawing furrows and fleeting palm prints. We thought of ourselves as sisters, or even daughters, instead of mothers, because it was with trepidation, that we had offered her our palms. Then the fortuneteller entered a secluded garden. And with each glance, she drew closer to a rhapsody of mysterious hordes. She watched us talk to the dead, pray upon their graves, and cover them with sunflowers. She saw us repeat those endless proverbs from the Talmud and the New Testament. But most of all, she saw us bound together with that familiar braid of infancy. At the entrance to a forgotten house, she looked at me, or at herself, rooted in the final seas. She saw us pass through every door and passageway, like eager, winged, creatures. And while she observed all of this, she foretold our joy, confused our palms, and perspired in the face of so much love.

My mother and I love each other wildly. We visit fortunetellers and astonish the future. Her palm is my palm. That life line belongs to her. And on my birthday, that is why it is the most precious gift.

WEDDINGS

I

We were married in August when the summer looked like a blanket of yellow moss. You gave me a bouquet of orchids. But I wanted yellow sunflowers like the flowering heart of the south. I wore an organdy dress, and inside, my pubis was a swarm of crimson. We married twenty years ago in order to comply with certain rituals, but not out of duty or tradition. We exchanged gifts. You gave me a ring that crumbles now in my hands of mist.

We celebrate many years of silent marriage. I don t count up the seasons, or the dead children, and familiarity brings us closer and closer to speechlessness. Sometimes I feel like a deranged mannequin inside a display window or a trunk of sequestered stories. I love you just the same. Naked, I approach your silence and your body.

II

We hold hands with the same innocence, perversity or custom of twenty years ago. Still fearful, we believe that keeping the secret of silence and uttering only a few words is the best way to love each other.

You ask me to lie next to you like an empty, lethargic, she-snail heeding the rhythm of absence. I must not speak, I am only to exist as a foundation or net. And thus, our children were born, fruits of the silence of an unspoken passion. That was how it happened, secretly, patiently, winking a tiny eye at God.

Today, without promises or tokens, we celebrate long years of silent marriage. Once more we have chosen the weight of silence, the dire hush of the forest, as if to take pleasure in chloroform dreams, or to nod beneath a tree in this plenteous season where the day approaches to mingle with the night. Where time begins to transform its vestments.

We walk toward the forest, this woods at summer s end. There are no poppies or sunflowers, like the meadow where you kissed me and I leaned forward to listen closer to the cadence of the wind. We hold hands as we always do, renewed by this ever present act of love which comes before all that is unchanging.

Today is our anniversary. I put on an organdy dress, silver earrings, and a gardenia. I marry you once again. Silently, I am happy.

WANDERERS
CHAPTER III

IN SEPTEMBER, WHEN THE RAIN STOPS

Before the rains stopped she was already dreaming about the sea lavishing its small caresses and reverberations of love around her ankles. She used to begin by taking out her summer clothes that smelled of the narrow solitude of confinement. She liked the straw hat she had purchased at the Arab s store because he told her that its winged shape looked good on her and covered up her freckles and pointy nose, diminished now by the misdemeanors of loneliness.

She would also take out the yellow beach bag where she meticulously kept her gloves of reddish lace and a towel to cover up her legs that displayed the ingratitude of time. Nonetheless, she dreamed of the sea, and often felt her moistened skin. She was hopeful thinking about the water, imagining herself naked through the windows of that seaside retreat, surrounded by gulls and the umbrellas of the impoverished travelers who came each year for a few days of sun. Then the boy with the fragile, unraveled body would come near her. He went to the water to rejoice in himself, to drown himself, or perhaps to die, perturbed and erect with love.

At times she dreams of him, and in the month of April when the earth flowers once again, she takes out her only organdy dress, knots her hair, and with ample hands, she sketches him, making tattoos around his mouth. Love, and the simple cruelty of desire fill her with light.

She is alone now and has grown smaller and smaller. When she wakes up she is very tiny and hunched over, as though time itself had made slits in her quartz and amber skin, blemishes; unpredictable and fleeting.

More than her ravaged body, she is afraid of loneliness, and the room that looks into a cellar filled with bats. And yet, that is where she evoked certain aromas and devious dreams. But now, everything inside her was incantation, fiesta, and water. Now the September rains were departing, and she would travel on the bus that takes the poor to the coast and arrive at that last seaside retreat with her blue satin suitcase and her hat. And way before she reached the beginning of the shoreline, she would sense she had brought him back to life by inventing him with her hands, as if he were made of plaster. Then she would return to ancestral love, to those cobalt blue goblets shared in a room of that great house where she dreamed she was beautiful, and the sea gulls nested in her pubis.

This time, no one is waiting for her and she makes her way toward the hotel whose shutters are starting to fall off. She is overtaken by an odor of rotten fish. But she is happy close to the sea celebrating and caressing her. It has been such a long time since anyone told her she was pretty or tasted of lavender. The old ladies from every summer are not waiting for her either. They teeter back and forth like mad, lonely, women talking to themselves about the latest rains and the face of loquacious innocence. And some of them only remember the birthdays of the dead, but she is content close to the sea, and the sun, that darkens her transparent skin.

She thinks of him and sketches him with minute and feverish hands. She waits for him outside on the terrace or in the room of invisible windows because it is summer and the rains have yet to arrive, and her body is a limp chain of flowers. She hears someone knocking at her door. It is the wind undressing her, and only the sound of water that envelops her on this evening that might be a day, or time uncertain. On this evening that marks the beginning of her years as a woman all alone.

The Alphabet

When Eduvijes Antipán Nahuenhual began to write, so began the enslavement of the letters. A native of the Cuatín River in the farthest region of the araucaria trees, Eduvijes did not master the sometimes doubtful capacity to write. She used to see the letters blink up at her from fashion magazines. But she couldn t put them together or make a chain of stories out of them or even in spite of them.

The letter "A" with its open and plentiful roundness reminded her of her perpetual births and the first cry of life everlasting. The dot on the "i" overwhelmed her with nostalgia, and the letter "l", made her eyes flutter until she blushed. Those were the only letters Eduvijes Antipán was able to repeat like a weary and dangerous song.

When a handful of missionaries and the infernal Germans from that cryptic past arrived in Chile, they began to teach Eduvijes the secrets of the alphabet as she squatted unashamedly to scrub huge bargefuls of crooked clothing that belonged to the village priests.

On the day she learned to read, the ladies with gray, mouse colored capes arrived from the ocean. The mayoress of the sea also came, bringing with her tiny sea lion pastries, not to mention the indispensable little priests who brought with them an extremely fat, potbellied blue bible. That is when Eduvijes bid farewell to her domestic chores. But before she left, she ironed Friar

Landislao s last set of curtains and fed the chickens and the plants. Then she gave everyone her address so they could write to her, and started out on her journey.

When Eduvijes returned to the Cautín region, she was unable to enter her modest adobe home. Letters blocked the door and windows. The local mailman lay dying. He could no longer keep up with all the letters she had received. There were love letters, letters of penitence, letters of rage, and even letters of relief. The most hair-raising fact about this occurrence was that along with her dubious spelling, and her use of the bible as a dictionary, she was fated to spend the rest of her life answering letters. She grew old and deaf writing letters and sending telegrams that read, letter to follow. Never was she able to see the yellow grass of autumn or watch the migrations of the birds. She was a woman held captive by the wisdom of the pen and the obligation of words.

DUNEDIN

Sunrises at Dunedin make me think of when the fireflies wake up. Delicate and fluttering, they begin to blink their eyes as if to turn on their fire at the first morsel of love. Then, after feverish nights of cadences and mists, they grow weary. In Dunedin the world seems to hang close to the sky and the houses have wings as if they too wished to be climbing angels. Karen Black lives in one of those houses and to the people of Dunedin she is known as the albatross queen.

Karen Black is British. Nevertheless, due to her scorn for an erstwhile love, she arrived in New Zealand at the age of seventeen and single-handedly devoted herself to operating the tour boats on the bay. And on days of glorious sun she takes the visitors to the hill of the albatross, a truly unique place in the universe. There, you can observe these gigantic and fantastical birds and truly journey across the skies on great wings, your body aloft, turning a gaze, and flight itself, into celebrations of love.

Karen Black knows the birds. She has been imagining them now for years. They say she makes sketches of them in her home when she returns from the boats. She knows the exact time at which they hasten to earth to drink the pure and crystalline water. She also knows when they are no longer in love and crash happily against the rocks.

From the moment they are born and commence their long flight, Karen Black makes sketches of the birds. Each evening she places the drawings next to her bed. And she herself seems to be a resplendent siren on earth presiding over the rhythm of the albatrosses.

It is said that Karen Black is peculiar. Sometimes she emits the moans of birds and her body, failed in its winged perfection, seems more and more prepared for unspoken and immediate flight.

It is said that in dreams, Karen Black looks like an albatross. Her body is spread out and sleeping. The depths of her hands are wide open. They say she sleeps on her back as if preparing herself for a journey.

They say that now and again it is possible to see her arise right at the beginning of dawn and turn the lights on in the city of Dunedin. Naked, she approaches the boats with her body of stone and moist breasts. She is filled with joy because she keeps watch over the arrival of the albatross, king of the heavens and hell.

IRELAND

She liked to repeat the word Ireland, with its cadences of R's, and sounds like those of an iris flower, or the rose of remembrance. She always said she would go to Ireland to see if it was as green as the pastures in her dreams and the chlorophyll green of leaves.

She liked to imagine herself enraptured and invisible on the coast of Ireland, making drawings through the rain, watching the ships without any sailors, and only the wind to cover her body that trembled before the murmur of the sea and the beating heart of the coast.

The history books said that her country was like Ireland, especially in the green and rainy south. Likewise, the father of her country was Irish, a man named O'Higgins, who freed the nation from the twisted yoke of bothersome Spain. Although history didn't interest her, what she wanted most was to feel the word Ireland, and be able to understand it in all of its innocence and insanity.

When her mother decided to build an attic to store her sewing things and some toys, as well as certain old love letters, she thought of the Irishman with his aroma of journeys who arrived at her house. She loved his green eyes that looked like the eyes of the meadows and woods. She loved his mischievous mouth that flowed with laughter and foreign sounds.

So great was their desire for each other, so many were

the wide-eyed glances, their eyes making the halo of a kiss, that the Irishman worked for years on the attic. He brought the wrong windows, useless doors, brittle skylights, only to prolong being next to the woman who was no longer small. Quite the contrary, she was getting bigger, and in between the planks of wood she was doing just the opposite of shrinking in order to celebrate her ever-increasing beauty.

For years, within the rubble of the attic, they would secretly become entangled. They made love searching for a place to rest from the absence after love. And she would ask him to sing songs and tell her what was behind the shadow of a forest. He was clever with words, measuring them with the precision of a carpenter or a maestro in the art of constructing noble spaces. And when he built the first skylight, he explained to her that questions were not as important as finding the path of migratory birds, looking with the silence of the eyes, and listening to the passing of death in her mossy hair that seemed like an ever-changing dawn.

When he was finally able to rebuild the door, he told her about the invisible elves and their green suits, perching themselves upon the origins of smoke. He told her that music and rain redeem themselves and that only within silence can one learn to remember.

For the Irishman, love was not saying words. It was feeling his body over the texture of hers inside a wordlessness inhabited by silence. Love was discovering a garden of green thicknesses, being weightless among the meadows, and sleeping all alone. But she asked him for words, and all he gave her were the offerings of a marvelous, enchanted attic which seemed like a soul at rest. She offered him her silent, unfurled body like something harvested in poverty that becomes fruitful.

The day came when the construction was finished and her mother kept her honorable word to pay the corresponding amount. The girl knew this and had become immense. She bade farewell to the Irishman. She called to him in a low voice but realized after he departed that she too had reached Ireland in her own spirited boat. Alone and ancient, at last she understood the mysteries of the Irish coasts and the magical rainbows, which she had finally been able to see from the attic. She saw the empty docks, her beloved descending in silence from a tiny lighthouse, wordless like the elves who cast spells with the colors of the forests and the quiet sounds of unspoken words.

CHOCOLATES

During her childhood, she was fanned with pheasant plumes when she woke up, and her body was bathed in iguana oil brought from the Isthmus of Tehuantepec. She was happy knowing that she was the mistress of the butterfly forest and a few infinitesimal stars. For years, she spent most of the day in her room surrounded by an entourage of beautiful damsels with sky-blue necklaces in their belly buttons. And although the country that witnessed her birth was reserved and snowy, and had nothing to do with a thousand and one nights, her father was of Egyptian origin and loved the idea of dreaming that perhaps one day he might be able to possess more than one woman. Nonetheless, he fell hopelessly in love with Raimunda and her protruding breasts, proprietress of the Andean district of the Araucaria trees and three glaciers. He found refuge in her luxurious bosom that looked like sweet custard, and was content to think about his harem and the truculent cemeteries of Cairo, that ideal place of rest.

The girl reached puberty. She was given lessons on how to walk and smile, and how to adorn herself with limp silk gloves. She was delicate and unassuming, and carried with her a legacy of the pride of the righteous. Furthermore, her life was to have a plan and be ordained by fate.

A sturdy whaleboat captain landed in those territories from the Islands of Nantucket, who, due to a peculiarity of childbirth, wished to see the likeness of things in that lost land where silence howls back at itself on icy, miserable evenings. When they met, they swore to love each other madly like the intoxication of that inhospitable calm. He offered her a house on the island of the whales that heaved in the gigantic expanse of the murky evening. He promised her roof gardens that would reach as far as the most exuberant dome of heaven. And it was on those very roof gardens that the woman learned the games of widowhood, those salutations without reply, on that lost island like the one in her beloved south, there, where glaciers are the mirrors of the sea.

Being so far away made her become more and more miserly with her words. She forgot her language and so forever lost the sounds of every river in her homeland. Nevertheless, she had always been a forgiving person and would remove the books of God from her butterfly basket and wish she might have been the Virgin Mary, owner and author of the universe.

As the seasons passed, the sturdy whaleboat captain met his fate at sea, and his widow was left more adrift than any shipwreck. She packed her scarce belongings, but was unable to return to her homeland. And so, clothed in the froth of the sea and her violet colored shoes, she left for another state in that remote New England land which she also could not feel as her own. Ever since the servants had ceased to perfume her body and she no longer felt the weight of gardenias and wild lilies upon her ears, she was at last able to comprehend that she was from nowhere. She was like those women of smoke who arrive unexpectedly at every gathering and prefer the silence of mists and the abundance of solitudes.

When she reached the surly coast of Maine in search of a placc to resι her vanquished body and her heart which was no longer wild, she met Mrs. Waterford, who rented her a small room above her chocolate shop. In the evening she felt contented, bathed in the sweet fragrance of vanilla, cinnamon, mints from Ireland, and French walnut confections. The aroma would rise up and fill her with light, drawing her far away from the shadows. Then she would sleep a divine and placid sleep.

Mrs. waterford was a shy and dignified woman. She had grown aloof from the contant task of kneading dough to make the chocolates, and from dreaming so many dreams that foretold recipes to her, both ancient and new. The old woman was able to acquire the peace and tenderness of those enamored of that succulent brew. And when she looked at Mrs. Waterford, she exuded a delightful sense of tranquility which reached the depths of sadness, and made the disinherited laugh.

On Fridays when the village swelled with summer people and fugitives, Mrs. Waterford never forgot the old woman who still wore tattered lace gloves to go shopping or play an imaginary game of croquet. Then she would open the door to her abode and let her come in. And while the old woman slept, Mrs. Waterford would give her the most extraordinary chocolates of every color, all wrapped up in tiny papers which were more like magic than the truth itself.

That is how the old woman learned the habits of love and the delectable alchemy of taste. She didn t have to hide behind screens to wait for lost sea captains or let the wretched servants dress her. At last, she could be happy, and be herself. Because all she had to do was reach her hand inside a straw butterfly basket to feast upon those milk chocolates with sugared almonds. Just being able to rub her mouth with that sweet elixir was enough to make her satisfied and feel love once again. And she knew that a generous hand was always held out to her, a hand without fear, and only a dozen chocolates, all wrapped up in tiny papers that were more like magic than the truth itself.

THE WANDERER

She is not a woman of habit. She prefers incongruence and the drowsy extravagance of disorderly things. She likes to explore the rhythm of invisible animals and makes note of the trajectory of bees and squirrels. Each morning she takes a walk in no particular direction almost touching the depths of trees. She walks quickly and boldly. Sometimes she mingles with the shadow of the air, but she likes to walk on her tiptoes. When the day gathers together with the sky, she is happy. That is when she starts off on her most abundant and deepest walk. She does this as a kind of grave and sacred mission because it is only during those moments that she becomes who she is, a walker, a woman who walks, making petals with the rhythm of her feet.

For weeks now, everyone has been watching her. They also see her pass by with that haphazard quickness. Winged beings, they all wait for her, knowing the hour of her return and the exact time she turns a corner that looks like the sky. She feels them watching her, banging on her heart. But they are not sure if it really her or the gaze of the other beings.

She senses that they would like to take her captive, but she does not know if it is the places of light in the woods, or the gazes or the other beings.

She has been walking for ten years or ten days. Someone shouts heinous epithets and vexations at her. They say they will come for her, that she must not walk or get tangled up with the time of the trees or the lilies.

She trembles not knowing if is the wind or that premonition announcing that perhaps they will come for her, because it is her duty to walk, to walk wildly, as if stood on end by the wind. When she reaches the corner that touches the sky, they call out to her. Her voice now has the sound of a prisoner, but no one covers her eyes or her voice, they merely look at her. These are women who do not understand how it is possible for a female wanderer to exist in those places where only cars pass by; where no one touches the air s breath or goes out of their house, where no one has time or an age, or says anything. All they do is look at her. She is in a frenzy and begins to knock upon her feet. She does not hesitate. She shakes the air and sunflowers from her knees and runs. This time, she does not walk. She cannot detain herself, and the rest of them follow after her because there are no sidewalks for their steps.

ISLANDS

When we reached the island we were like uninhabited souls, ghosts of beings thrust below the darkness of a threatening, and yet alluringly sinister evening. The night sky loomed above us like a great ocean prison where stars barely foretold their paths. Tiny lamps glowed in two or three shops, making them look more like funeral parlors than a place where old drunks used to dream the dream of death and indifference.

With steps of foreboding and sweet fear, I drew closer to the enormous winged night. Everything was hollow and shapeless until we reached the island house beyond the sea tides, far from the salt knolls and the odor of life. We would always arrive intoxicated by fear and pleasure.

Antonia Pérez, empress of adobe and naked earthenware, somberly greeted us. But her smile reflected the dark halls of thousands of dead souls. And then, in the shadow of a house that smelled of moss and sadness, we also drank warm and bitter wine.

I dreamed I was inside a beautiful, ill-fated painting and a magnificent fire from the nearby chimney made me remember those soaring flames of love and the funeral pyres of death. I imagined I was a adolescent locked in an old man s house by the sea.

We were on an island of rocky Pacific coasts, and yet, we couldn t hear the sound of the ocean or see the blue from the sky. Everything was vieled in an immaculate silence. Even the old man s breathing couldn t be heard next to my ear. I wasn t sure if he was the desire of an imaginary man, or a plain s wolf, following me through the golden nightmares of my childhood. I knew nothing, only that I was held captive between the footprints of the forest and the overpowering protection of the sea.

He came close to my body, holding me beneath a solitude like the rituals after love making. I had no notion of silences or the tides, only his body drawing tattoos on mine. Then I learned that his body and essence were like a village of tiny streets where one could hide or begin a conversation full of entrances and exits. They have spoken to me about running away. But, why should I flee? I like the old man s body stretched out on top of mine because it looks like a chicken, innocent and mutilated. So tender is his skin, that I feel I am holding a newborn baby in my arms. How I love this breathless wordless silence, his body over mine, and the rocking of the sea waiting to pull us down into its velvet texture.

I am disturbed, out of my head, bound to this love, to this old man who approaches me. It is pleasure that takes possession of time, and I promise to write more about him, although six red roses have now bloomed in the forest, and I don t know how I will tell him about it.

After we came to the island, I never departed from it. My body became a blanket of water and a promise. Ilusive waves came nearer and nearer to the room. We are happy . He is dying in his sleep. And I awaken in the death of that love.

OCEAN RETREATS

I

Although brittle and consumed by the passage of time, like a maimed butterfly, she draws near the summer as if it were love.

II

It is said that when she was next to the sea, she used to close her eyes the way young lovers came to listen to the essence of the deep at the very end of the century.

III

In the summer she likes to cover her body with tattoos, and her navel is a verdant raft where the birds nest. In the winter when the rains begin to surround her, she takes out her compasses and nautical cards and selects the ocean constellations to cover up the mirrors. Then, like a beast, she quietly advances toward the summer on those days when the rains make a circle around her.

From constantly staring at herself naked in the mirror, she grew into a magnificent pillar of salt, an exquisite shipwrecked woman arriving at every shore.

She always chooses the same dilapidated hotel because they take care of her ragged beach umbrella and worn-out hat. They remember her year after year and keep an eye out for her rusting skin while she is away. She is thrilled to have them wait for her and cover her with soft shawls filled with holes. Summer has come at last, and she is no longer alone.

I like the summer
because I leave the earth
to go inside the water's
deepest place
and I am only sorry
I never went inside your eyes.

ALLISON

I

Allison approaches, disappears behind the thresholds, she is, is not, a sleepy shadow, a woman from a dark and innermost place like the twilight of something treacherous and remote. I like Allison because she laughs, and in her laughter it is easy to sense that she has spoken with death, contemplated her body dressed in a skeleton, felt remorse, and then changed her mind in favor of the gestures of life.

II

I am fond of Allison's house because it is full of clocks which don't even tell time or the seasons, only the progression of the dead who carefully draw near at certain hours of the afternoon or in the fear of the night when Allison sets places of happiness for them at the table of dead souls.

III

Allison's furniture seems to have lived at the ocean because it has the deep texture of moist things and the roughness of salt, as though ready to be shipwrecked. Nontheless, it resists the damage of anger, memory, and haste. The walls of her house are pink and purplish-red and have golden doors where Allison often walks through secret passages as if transfixed, her face colored with stars in order to ask the dead about lost things, braids of garlic, oregano, and golden bracelets.

Allison's house smells like herbs and cemeteries, and these fragrances become entangled, but she has an aroma of love and what we begin to love. Nothing is more frightening than to enter a house with no smells. Houses, those little mausoleums where we build our conscience, predict and preach about fate, the dying, and newborn babies.

I like Allison's eyes. They are like two ferocious belly-buttons, effervescent, always gleaming, holding closely to the docks and the texture of water. And she laughs with the voice of a shipwrecked woman, a sea captain's voice, and goes to meet the portals of her home.

DEATH SOUNDS
CHAPTER IV

THE PLACE I WANT TO DIE

Death came to sit at the edge of my bed as if she herself were surrounding a dream of liquid depths. I liked the violet tulle she wore. She was young like me and terribly enamored of life. I was half-asleep, and any communication with her seemed useless. But I wanted to ask her where, and what time she would come for me. I wanted to know if by chance she would be arriving during the languor of the drought season, or perhaps while I was walking in a plaza or deserted park.

My dream did not overflow with anguish, only penetrating curiosity. For instance, I would want to know if my parents would still be alive to cover up the mirrors the way sad people do who are filled with immense grief, or if my husband was going dress my feet with my parents red shoes.

Death grew tired of watching me and placed her ever so feeble hand across my forehead. And with a kiss made from the aromas of wild woods, grass, and confinement, she bade me farewell. That same evening I decided to write her a letter because I was curious about how and where to die. For example, it wouldn t be very fashionable to die with a chicken bone caught in my throat, runs in my stockings, or my hair all messed up. Wouldn t it be exquisite to die in the arms of a handsome, older man in a house with violet lamp posts looking out at an imaginary sea? Wouldn t it be beautiful to die at the age of ninety after a plenteous night of love?

My friend René told me she wanted to die in a small village. A place where everyone remembers you and throws flowers in your path when you pass by. Then I imagined I would like to die in Rousillion, in southern France. Now, don t think I am a snob. I like Rousillion because the houses are violet, like the garb of death. When someone dies, the old men from the Plaza bring yellow butterflies and have a chirping contest. Then they sing the Marseilleses and Lily Marlene . That s the way I want to die. So they ll sing to me with voices of birds and cover me in lavender.

LADY DEATH

She has been coming to visit me for a long time. She has a frail look about her, as if she were tired of bluffing or never able to decide exactly when it will be my turn to accompany her to the room of the maimed guests. I have grown used to her censureless presence, notwithstanding certain slight movements, similar to those of clandestinity. I like her wardrobe of tulle and gauzes of sea colored dark bluish-purples, and her winged gloves.

I think she looks like a thin, sinister, angel, but an angel, nonetheless. Perhaps she is an agile player of cards and fortunes. However, her presence gives me great tranquility. I have become familiar with her steps. She always arrives after midnight as though she had just departed from a quiet and prudent dance. She comes close to me and tries to caress me, but I do not allow her any sort of confidentiality. I know she waits for me, but I refuse to give her even an inch of my closeness. I do not want her to see my naked body in a vulnerable position. I do not wish for her to intrude upon my face down dreams. I only ask for her patience, and that she wait for me. Because I still have several dances to attend, especially the dance of the grief-stricken masks. I still need to fix the roof, although I enjoy sleeping face up and very close to the rain.

It is hard for me to talk. I grow speechless with fright and happiness because I don t know when I ll have to depart. I would prefer to leave the roses pruned, the handkerchiefs and love sheets ironed, and watch that movie I was saving till the last. Besides, I d like to have a huge party filled with sweet nectar, orange blossoms, and beloved friends. And I d like to have a room for discoveries. A place where I could keep all the objects found inside those read and re-read love letters, and all the jewels lost in parks, not to mention the party.

I don t know if she will wait for me. I can see her impatiently scratching her nose. I sense that she thinks I am demanding. But I am only asking for two more days. One more day of air, one last sigh.

RIVERS

I love rivers with their lush texture, algae color, and their sayings about death. Rivers are like life, brimming with flower garlands, red-purple fiestas, anemones, and fanciful circles.

The river is an honored place for love, behind or above the water. You and I beneath the water, in hideaways of gathered rock, enraptured, filled with love and rage, fleeing, yet always approaching the river.

In the river, marine creatures, mollusks, swordfish, and turtles all make love. For this is also the place where they find each other. Because the river has walls and boundaries, drawing the confines of history, geography, and the course of events.

In the river people look at each other and wait. They watch boats bearing fruit and news. Boats bearing the dead, and dresses for brides.

In my country, women peer into the river to gather skeletons and bones transfigured into fish. The river brings the soul after insomnia. It brings and the ever bright and noble face of a tortured human being.

The river is like the regions of life. But it conspires with death when waters cease to flow, bringing drought and grief inside a landscape that is history.

The river also sings and tells. It looks like arms or ponds, or fertile islands where people gaze at each other and grow tender. Rivers without borders are like death, only an illusion, only a tiny ration of water.

ANTIGUA

He had chosen that city of cobblestones and rose petals as if to flee from themselves and from desire. They had chosen Antigua, in Guatemala, because someone told them about that odd and flower-laden springtime. They had also been told about the dead who, like stranded mermaids, had no graves or markers. They were told of the meadows filled with copal, and the bodies that were traitorous to desire itself. And then, as if intoxicated, they set off on their journey with that silence of invisible passions, ominous and beautiful, like the flame of God.

Now and again he would look at her to reassure himself that she was at his side. And they remained like that all through the everlasting evening, crouched upon the root of a dream like enchanted lovers who meet each other beneath the sigh of vulnerability and shared dreams. They gaze at each other and their words are a shadow between clouds appearing like cities unearthed.

The city loomed before them like a colossal expanse of plentiful, distorted time. The old narrow streets followed the curve of dreams, and the swallows had an aroma of wild wood and the tiny openings in rose petals. On that listless and sinister afternoon nothing was moving. They had reached Antigua, a handsome city, disfigured by the years, slaughtered upon the deepest place in its countenance. Someone guided them through those remote spaces even though no one inhabited that city, which had been plundered by history, human beings, and animals. The city seemed to move as if everything were strangled and hushed.

They arrived at the Santo Domingo Hotel, illuminated only by the shimmering face of the candles that rocked back and forth to the beat of an even more strangled wind. In that quiet and scheming darkness they began to desire each other. Their faces also became disfigured by that city, which all of a sudden had lost every one of its rose petals. He slowly licked her hair, making small chains of dead roses for her neck, telling her again and again that he loved her with the solace of fugitives and the reckless. She could only imagine great dove hands, hands which seemed to be born from within her forehead.

"Why do you moan?" he asked. "What loneliness do you hold within your breath?" She answered that at last in that city of barefoot people and dead souls, in that tiny, humble city she had found the happiness of desolate villages. They stayed awake all night in a nudity beyond love, when lips remain half-open, near the aroma of wood.

He told her he liked her silence, imagining her body as if it were the city itself, darkened by the evening, as if her abdomen and hands were places of shelter for absent passers-by. He told her to stay in that position, barefoot, her breasts suspended by the air's slow caresses, and the rain, which seemed to come from very deep within their bodies.

When it drew closer for a kiss, they would move further

away. And in that elegant hotel, death's illicit comings and goings perched upon the entrance to the room with crackling candles and a smell of scorched death.

It was the first time they had been together in seven years, and he was not timid about the movements of love or feeling her body give off a fragrance of timber, wild grass, and undeniable love-making. And they held themselves in that tangled closeness, as if to keep death in the distance, as if, in that bed, in that southern place filled with rose petals and maguey, death itself could forever remain buried in the wet earth.

It was dawning. Her hair was growing without any seaweed, and was verdant and ashen. They were awakened by a noise, and for a moment they were not sure if they had reached heaven, punished for their desire of love. But then they remembered they were in the very ancient city of La Antigua, and the scent of roses was coming from the people and the cries of the market just beginning its daily rituals.

They were told that during the night the city had also fallen into a spiral-shaped dream of peace and color, and the dead had gone out for a walk on the cobblestones, scattering sacks of yellow roses, candles and maize all about.

WARNINGS

Shortly before the hour of her death, my great-grandmother, Helena, from Vienna and a neighbor of Martin Buber, requested that the mirrors be covered in purple-red tulle brought from the sullen baskets of war. She selected a starched white dress, confusing it with the nuptials of her premature engagement. She undid her hair and awaited the desired vigil, those sweet but undeniable seizures, like omens from a winged forest of fireflies.

Since my father was a doctor, he was the one who closed her eyes. And she returned to Bavaria and Goethe, to an Austria brought back to life only in her memory.

When death came to my father's room on crumbling heels forty years after Grandma Helena died, we felt it as something foreboding and perverse because it happened so unexpectedly, and it wasn't his turn or his time. Death came as if to serve notice that she would take him away again in a moment, an hour, or even in twenty more years. And she branded us with a poison tattoo.

Since then we haven't been the same. We do not forget her. And now we are like an almanac that keeps a record of the strange and hollow steps of death.

For a few moments, my father lost his voice and one of his arms. His tongue returned to an expanse of silence as he listened to a fugue from Bach. They carried him away, unconscious.

When he returned from the forest and was able to eat or utter words, when the tickle on his tongue became a swarm of honey once again, we were thankful. I remember Grandma Helena said that everyone's hour is written in the book of life which is the memory of God. So I decided to write a story about my father and celebrate the miracle of God.

SPIRITS

It makes no sense to ask what region or landscape witches inhabit. I advise you to imagine that they are everywhere. On bright days, it is easy to watch them passing clearly through the graveyard, dining with the dead, or striking up endless conversations with the spirits. Spirits are people whose yearning for happiness has not been fulfilled. That is why they meander about, vacant and in disarray. They come in through bedrooms, sprawl themselves out against the walls, and dream about happiness.

Witches serve as guides and companions for spirits because they are both visible and invisible. Sometimes witches help the spirits celebrate their passage into the hereafter. They also teach them that finding joy is simply a matter of looking at the dome of the sky, or watching the clouds draw figures of elves across the starry expanse.

Evening arrives swiftly and mischievously. And I become permeated with aromas. Around me, everything is in bloom. It is a clear and beautiful day. Then the witches arrive. They tell me secrets. They are wise and powerful, they prepare brews in clay kettles. The wind blows unwary behind the balustrade. The fog makes us sing out of fear. The witches are there, like beacons or genies, or gleaming souls. I love them because they tell my fortune. Then they caress me, and make me understand the fear of happiness.

HOUSE OF LIGHTS

I liked the house. From the outside it seemed to be peaceful and filled with the light like something enchanted. We enjoyed taking walks around those presumably unrefined gardens, which, upon closer examination, were perfectly taken care of. The bushes were planted in such orderly fashion as to seem almost sinister, and brilliant care was taken of those shining leaves which appeared to be the evil dreams of chloroform.

With longing we used to think that one day we would like to live in that house and watch the sun or the air descend from those small windows which faced the last domain of a forest situated at a crossroads.

The owners of the house were a small, chubby couple who seemed to be fairly prosperous, existing within a harmonious self-centeredness. As soon as the sun came up she could be seen watering the bushes with a reddish-purple liquid and when the doors were closed, the outline of an unusual light was always visible. For years the neighbors would observe that the couple followed an ancient routine. And when the sun began to return each day, when darkness gives us permission to contemplate certain secrets and certain deceiving gestures, the couple would hide themselves away in that house on the hill, far from the voices of others.

The couple who lived in the house of lights always wore the same clothing and time remained still on their faces. They smiled sparingly and only appeared to be content when they watered the shrubs with that reddish-purple liquid. They lived for many years in our small country next to the sea and the mountains. People disappeared. Children disappeared. Houses were painted a deep gray cement color. The color of fear. The color of grief. For many years we weren't allowed to go out on our balconies, and we sank beneath a spell of misfortune. Despite all this, the couple was happy and took advantage of those regulations by never going out of their house. No one saw them for a long time, until the mailman brought them a religious card from Rome which had wings on it and seemed to be able to fly. Only then was it apparent that now no one lived in the house of lights. As if by some unseen gesture they no longer existed. Even the faces of that sensible couple could no longer be seen near the house. Nonetheless, the house was white and radiant as if it had been cleaned to perfection by silent spirits. And the bone of cleanliness could be seen there. But not the bone of death. The owners of the house had disappeared as if they themselves were part of the bewitching space that used to live inside of them. We moved to the house with one small bed and my mother's wooden divan.

Ever since the dawn of the first day we moved, the house began to fill up with dust. It penetrated the doorways and beyond the labyrinths. This swift and evil dust was moving through our bodies and killing the winged space of our sleep. That maddening dust wasn't allowing us to live, nor did the lights which constantly went out, making us fall into very dreariest of darknesses.

Weeks later I became sick from insomnia. A migraine

headache was hounding me like an attack dog or a beast. A season of evil had descended upon me. Someone was scratching my skin and my skirt, and at times we sensed that death had us surrounded. She was an amicable lady, yet anxious and clean. And she looked like the floor in the house of lights. Around us, nothing bloomed, and the perfect shrubs would die off at the crack of dawn only to come to life again during the bitterness of the evening.

When it was nearly impossible for me to walk, we departed and so recuperated our words and the rhythm and gift of love. When we used to take walks around the house of lights, sometimes, in through the window we could perceive a faint light, the dust and the shrubs, lively and beautiful, blossoming in the sunrise.

WIDOWHOOD

From the time I was a little girl, I liked to pretend I was a widow, but not because of those frightening and very, very, dark veils that seemed like evil omens of the evening, I liked widowhood because that word had a flavor of elegance, mystery, and something remote. It made me think of those demure ladies with subtle gloves who gathered near the late afternoons to drink gin and Burmese tea. I remember my aunt, Zulema Esquivel, for example. Her bereavement was touching. She wore a very tight, pitch-black skirt, while smoking a cigarette that tasted more like opium and tranquility than any ordinary Marlboro.

I wanted to become a widow from the time I was a little girl. Perhaps that is the reason why my marriage transpired with uncommon normality. I met a decent gentleman. He wasn t an accountant or a barber. He had a small computer business, lots of gooey hair, and a fairly acceptable ancestry. I loved him somewhat, that is to say, at those times when passion easily mingles with rapture. I loved his silence and his belief in the future and the hereafter. We got married.

In the evening we made love and talked nonsense with dirty words on the other side of our ears, or at the very end of our buttocks. And when the sun came up, when the odor of gums and painful mornings covered us, I would realize that day by day I was getting closer to widowhood and the things of silence.

During the day, I cautiously went about my tasks. I would open the neighborhood beauty shop and dress up in a blackish, tight lace garment. Then I would go wild messing up long locks of hair and disentangling them, drawing tattoos on other women s heads. And I delighted in the delicate harm that could be heard coming from the red heads. I thought very little about my husband, and sometimes it took a superhuman effort on my part to remember his name or the day we had agreed to meet at the sweet shop. Little by little, the desire to be a widow took on a powerful share of the truth. I ate my ham and cheese all by myself. I told him not to speak to me at coffee time and not to go into my closet. I made him take all of his clothes out of there and only let him keep his boy scout hat in there. At night, we slept in separate bedrooms and even the sound of his breathing was beginning to make me feel anxious. I forced him to use our dog Bonito s, muzzle. He went along with all my tyrannical demands. He promised me he would let me go free very soon and that he would leave home. At last, in the prime of my life, I was thrilled to have reached widowhood without having to put up with him forever, without having to fold his socks or scratch his corns on rainy days.

I liked to pretend I was a widow from the time I was a little girl. But now that I am thirty-six and slowly falling into the details of life, now that it is getting difficult to hear the beating of my heart, being alone makes me happy. It s like putting on a black dress, lighting candles, celebrating insomnia, and wide, marvelous beds, just for dreaming, just for waking up feeling fresh without having anyone burp at me, or say stupidities to me in my middle ear, held in the boredom of a dismantled bed. At last, now I am a widow without a dead man.

APPOINTMENT

She used to spend time in zoos and was fond of hyenas and ferocious, nocturnal animals because she too was a stealthy being and had been born from a skin that was now growing more brittle each day. As time went on, she chose the loneliness of wild, barren lands making ocean currents out of deserts and trails anointed by the restless footprints of indifference. She did not approach the humanity of things or even the rituals of those eternal ceremonies of love.

She abandoned lace bodices and the caressing hand of her lover who drew circles through her wild skirt made from devious lace. For many years she settled for a life of penury and greed, and never knew how to allow herself to feel the songs of the river or the region's neighboring waters. She became old, putrid and faded. Baldness surrounded her, making her evermore wakeful and hazy eyes, even larger.

Death knew about her, and the nakedness which only drew near the surface of things made her uneasy. Often, she had seen her peeking from behind the balustrade as if confused and deflowered. Death liked her caved-in ankles, her freckles, her ostrich-feathered hat, and her decaying belly button. Sometimes death followed her on her decrepit journeys or perverted promenades through cities without oceans because she wanted to keep her fixed in her mind. Then she would know the exact moment at which she would recognize her and take her away to the shifting borders of mist and the rocky fringes of her kingdom.

For several months death visited her while she slept in her nakedness. It was still possible to observe certain translucent signs on her breathless leopard skin and lean baldness. The pantings of humanity falling away from her half-liquid, half-rigid skin could also be heard. Even in a dream it was possible to be frightened of her. Death had smiled at her once when she saw her unprotected, barefoot and resting peacefully. But she went berserk when she saw her stockings ironed and her suits in a perfect state of insanity. Then death knew that even in her daydreams she was greedy and weak. She began to think she would never again dream about forests or the mouths of rivers. She was sure that love had never disturbed the lips of that being with the magnitude of a sublime caress and also came to realize that she was cagey and exact, and had practiced rituals with the deceit of misers. Death meditated about these things and asked herself if it was worth it to take her away that same evening or allow her to live like a wounded bird without a flock.

Oddly, death had compassion for her. Nevertheless, it was a curious compassion. She sensed that removing this being to the spaces of twilight or the gruesomeness of shadows would bring her evil omens and the idleness that life has. She reasoned that having her present at the table of the dead would not be savory or worthwhile. Consequently, she decided not to wait. She put away the blue silk shroud, tied her witch's shoes, and made up her mind to punish her by giving her the possibility of eternal life. She would allow her to exist forever without any aspirations or finalities, only the raising of glasses at the very end of her life. Death had decided to allow her to live and had come to the conclusion that she was too perverse to be allowed to remain at the bottom of annihilation's exalted darkness. As a result of that decision, the town grave diggers had to suffer a little more.

Now, no one would have the pleasure of burying her inside her skeleton blanket of dry leopard. Now, no one would inherit the cabin made of stuffed vultures and empty sacks of moldy flour. Death had changed an appointment for the first time; she let her live forever. Then, she put on her silk stockings, her patent leather shoes, and departed in her carriage to search for a better, more generous companion.

DEATH SOUNDS

Death sounds, like a darkness that lies in wait at the center of emptiness. Death sounds, untimely, yet precise, making tiny sentences out of weeping and incantation.

So much silence in the room. So much memory hidden on wordless faces. They put in the nails and call out, forever sealing that subtle story, that unforgettable mosaic which separates the living from the dead and those who are now a memory of water.

The dead man is no longer cold or afraid. He makes himself comfortable in the gnawed wood. And while the body is being sealed off, the death sounds approach like maimed bells for the temperate ears of the living. Can t you hear them? Don t you see them?

They nail slowly to be certain that neither soul nor body will rise up over the tops of the trees. They call out to be certain that this allotted time on earth, as with all others, shall take its place on the very highest throne of irrevocable farewells.

Death sounds in the vastness of arid land. Death sounds like the steps of lonely women who leave no footprints in the snow or sounds to follow them in the desert.

And she asks them not to take him from the house, that the coffin remain a little longer. She asks them not to remove the nails so that once more he may light upon the sudden roundness of her arms. Like a blood searing echo, only the death sounds lie in wait for her. Have you heard the sounds of death when they come to visit us?

THE COLOR BLACK

Of all the imaginable colors and rainbows, black was the color she preferred because she loved funeral shrouds and funerals. Black was like the dark things in her soul placing a disguise over her extremely small, very close eyes. Black covered up her behind, which grew larger on weekends. And one could imagine the color black every Sunday as a sensible tablecloth on which to play a game of chess.

During the day she liked to wear plain black while taking her majestic promenades. She was very fond of evening funerals when the dead still carry the aroma and rhythm of the living.

She would select her favorite outfit; black underpants, the evening's gloomy measurements, a black leather purse and black leather roses. For her lipstick she chose a garnet color, which made her sharp and unpretentious moustache stand out. When she arrived at the funerals she spoke of death the way one gobbles up a plate of chicken with rice or a dish of flan spilling out all over. She took pleasure in talking about the dead and cried for them with the same insincerity with which she vowed to love the living. She wept, and on radiant days sometimes it was possible to see that the tears she wept were not made of salt or even water. On the contrary, they were made of tiny little putrid pieces of garlic which fell from her fleeting eyelids. As she wept, one could observe her protuberances; her breasts inflated with balloons and black wads of cotton, her stomach filled with black pork rinds and the spine of an old, scorched chicken.

There wasn't a funeral or a dead person who could stand her. At times, when married couples, brothers and sisters, or lovers would die, before they descended into that gentle region of death, they would talk among themselves and say, "Can you see that woman black who is weeping?" "She has come to fill us with her garlic smell." "The prophecies of bad fortune will visit upon us."

It didn't matter how often they played tricks on her, or how often everyone allowed her to cry her garlic tears all by herself, she was always there, omnipresent, spread out over the bodies, trying to see if she could find a ring or crown to show off at the next funeral.

TICKLE OF LOVE
CHAPTER V

REVENGE

It has been a long time now since I have been getting ready for revenge, both big and small. Don't worry, my desire to kill is not a powerful one. But a little revenge can be sweet and deliberate. It can cheer us up on those nights of sorrow and stomachaches. When I am bored and the cats urinate disastrously all over the roof, when the neighbors bang on the ceiling with witches' brooms, that is when I come to life, perfume myself all over, and dream about revenge.

I'll make a short list, like the ones for the supermarket, and the first item will be to poison my lover. Well, he used to be my lover on certain precocious and precautious evenings in hotels filled with devious professors. I'd like to poison him during a conference on semiotics. First we would go to have something to eat, and we would talk. I would tell him I am a postmodernist, and I'd show him my breast and my stocking, all crumpled up like an ice cream cone.

After the first two or three glasses of campari, I would notice that his tongue and his body had loosened somewhat. And we would proceed to a room in a hotel which is usually near an airport. Don't ask why, I have always stayed in airport hotels. Then, after we had penetrated each other's bodies, and not the laws of semiotics, I would remove an obviously poisoned chocolate from my Colombian leather bag (a gift from a mafioso), and I would say to him, "Here it is, my love, it's all yours."

Then, just like those scenes on stage or in horror movies, he would eat that chocolate, and I would watch him explode in pain. All through the night I would observe him next to my bed and he wouldn't need to run down the corridors of that airport hotel like a fugitive at two o'clock in the morning. I would observe him, dead, from contentment and sin. All night long he would hold me in his arms with that chocolate in between his almond eyes. Just for one evening, I would wish him eternal sleep. What I mean is, that just for once he would spend the night with me. He would rest his neck on mine, and his poison, chocolate breath would fall on top of my golden buttocks, drowsy from the sweet aroma of chocolate, love, and poison.

Sometimes, while my husband is sleeping, I'd like to put a soft little goldfish inside of him. And I'd like that tiny fish to tickle him next to his Adam's apple so I could have one evening without those marriage sounds. Without those burping sounds. Without those sounds of the television or radio. Don't you think that women my age deserve an evening of peace? One silent evening of love?

I have very few friends and prefer the life of a recluse. I am fond of cellars and closets. I don't like to answer the phone because it gives me a rash. I don't get along with the neighbors because they are fat in a masculine way and because I divide the world into obese women, witches, and evil men. That's my motto. And since chocolates are too expensive, I don't want to poison them, but I'd like it if they choked on their chicken. I don't want a bone to get caught in their husky throats.

But I'd like it if just for a moment, they were unable to swallow so they could comprehend the burden of silence and stop lording it over their compliant cooks.

I always ask myself what the perfect revenge against God might be. Taking sleep away from him or forcing him to copy children's prayers by hand? Requesting that he answer the letters written to him or telling him once and for all that he has been too much of a liar and we don't believe in him anymore? My revenge would be to tell God that it has been a long time since children didn't believe in him because on those evenings of war their dolls go up in flames and widows still weep on narrow streets of sorrow.

I explained to you that revenge does not have to be the task of witches. Revenge is desire colored by the tiny veins of love. Bring me a splendid little piece of chocolate. Bring me an icy chicken and a death notice to write this small letter to God.

FINGERTIPS

With the round lightness
of your fingers you
open my soulful heart
filling me with rhythms
of blue vessels and
watermelons of gold
with the round lightness
of your fingers you
open my soulful heart
and make me possessor
of your tongue.

THIS LOVE

I

In the evening, we awaken as if we had no arms or breath. In the evening, we awaken on a fragile threshold of foreboding. And in that silence of river and of air, we find each other. I feel your tongue approaching. It wraps itself around mine, and returns, as fortune does, to the hidden place of light where love is.

II

Only within nakedness, only in the aura of flesh were they able to feel at peace. They would hold their arms open and whimper. They were not thirsty or cold. Time, like a blue canvas, was all that existed, time to kiss each other in a basket full of swallows.

III

We didn t trade addresses or hazy gestures. We only lingered within the hushed uneasiness of the evening, enraptured, delirious, gazing at each other in order to cherish that inexpressible illusion of love. Two desperate bodies holding on to the warmth of closeness, recollection, and the memory of something unimaginable.

IV

Before writing to you, I perfume myself all over so I can talk to God.

V

While you are sleeping, or pretend to be the thankless wretch of sleep, I pause before your quiet hands which divulge a host of stories. In them, I see dead children, and the women you made love to, their guts torn open through the silence. All through the everlasting evening I draw closer to your hands which strangle and caress me. Out of them fall knives, shrouds, thimbles, and one enormous living heart. All night long, I hold myself in your hands as if wishing to climb them to reach the heaven, lingering inside of them, in order to talk to God.

VI

Over and over in their wayfaring, shipwrecked ears they tell each other they will never see each other again. They say they no longer desire each other, that restrained love is senseless when they are weary from hunger, cold and loneliness. He tells her he does not want her liquid breasts to rest against his emaciated, gleaming, legs, which are all alone like the autumn and its beginnings. She looks at him as if he were the very last pale bird to live through every insomnia. And she forgets her modesty and pride. She undresses him, and bites him, asking him again and again to kiss her and place his body over hers, as if his arms were able to create her moist thighs. Then she asks him to place his tongue very close to the throbbing heart of her pubis.

VII

Love. All love is like an illness or a tender, sweet tickle.

But more than anything, it is filled with light and rage. His love, or imagining where his love begins, is like a second skin, or a quiet, hidden, fear.

VII

Love; forbidden, secret, exquisite, taboo. Love in the mad cities of México, Quito, and Cuenca. In the cities it is always the same and always different. She is only able to remember the light piercing their naked bodies like a brilliant mask. She cannot feel her own body, or even his. She can only feel between her thighs. She only remembers the light passing through their bodies, soothing them. She only recalls the lights from the cities, shining on a face that is like every wary, cruel lover, like all lovers who meet in the churning secret of one tongue upon another.

IX

She pleads with him to remain naked and very close to her, immersed in an ancient silence. She feels his hands bathing her, drying her, and she is eternally happy knowing that his gaze replenishes her.

X

Your whole body is like a land that one returns to. Your hands are trees behind a shadow. Your tongue, the odyssey of silence, each limb, a beacon or a shore.

More than a repetition of the rituals of love, we are the dispossessed, the speechless, the ones who choose dangerous navigations- knowing that one never reaches a safe shore, only the uncertainty of a beating heart.

A SCENTED LOVE LETTER

I

I had intended to write you a love letter, perfume myself from head to toe, and take off all my clothes. With my voice and the vocations of my body, I had intended to make rituals, elusive paths, and the transparencies of love.

II

I had intended to draw you closer to invisible things; a nail from the body, cut to pieces, dreaming of itself, the last photograph of a snowy forest. I had intended to perfume those quivering intonations which remind us of secret openings, those journeys nestled by the intoxication of exhaustion. I had intended to perfume our ever gentle love making, that vaporous semblance of eternal music.

This letter is not for you or for me. The person who receives it will be an imagined or imaginary body, the desirable medium of some confused reader or insomniac.

III

I am writing this letter as a ritual of farewell. I am writing with indisputable steadfastness to calmly inform myself that it is far and away impossible for you to continue these restricted visits or to descend upon the fireflies of my body. The fact that my face matches your own, like the sigh of dead friends, or those garments with aprons of ash, is a piercing reality.

I am not writing this letter to feel sorry for myself or to curse you. I am writing simply to sharpen memory like the somber knives of wordless love lying upon a disturbed remembrance of the last dawn of the century. You shall no longer dry my flowing hair or tell me it is beautiful. I will no longer secretly dream of evening garments, sea gulls in the summer, peaceful bodies, or raging love.

More than indifference, you have taken away my illusion to continue to invent you, write love letters to you, or arrange those absent rendezvous. I am learning to comprehend your smallness, your incapacity to gravitate between the shadows of my pubis and then return, panting, to that brief tale of oneness. There was so much I learned and unlearned as I approached your distant and stifled gaze, made beautiful by one generous act: sharing with me a translucent crevice of your body in among the shadows.

Love letters are to be read out loud and hidden away in closets of the evening. And when this sequestered passion is aroused, one must hold the letters closely, pounding them against the walls of the heart, scattering them about, making love on top of them. But none of this is remotely possible. I am writing this love letter to congratulate myself. I have created a fabulous lover out of you, an ill-tempered gladiator, a knight-errant who always used to give me flowers and invisible musical harmony. Even though none of this was, or will come to pass, the truth is that I was in love with your liquid, glowing eyes because they were the very darkest places of all that remains open. I desired your simple nakedness, perturbed like a stolen adolescence. I loved your mute cadences and the curtains of a thousand hotels concealing us, making us safe in clandestine cities, lost in the only sacred place of the forgotten dominions of greed.

You are returning now to your proper place where nothing and no one remembers you. Those nights of only one wild heart, like my own, succulent and swollen upon your face, beating very slowly like a vessel of water, like a great city of peace and joy. Life has become easy for you. You don t have to lie. You think you have fallen back into that perverse domesticity of good marriages. You don t have to pretend to wash away the traces of love during those miserable homecomings. It was easier to make me disappear or think of me as an empty chair in some hotel room. But chairs can talk too. They tell their own stories. And behind the embossed tapestry lie radiant secrets.

I am writing this love letter to assure myself that I am a great storyteller, even though I never wore masks or ostrich-feathered lace. I was thirsty, a crazy woman who became sick with love when I would think of returning to your gaze or the turquoise corner of your back. When I held your aroma and the fleeting desire of your resilient, glistening penis between my legs, I was a raving beast.

I became larger from inventing you so often. And from loving you so much, I grew. I have recovered from all those uncertain good-byes. And now I bid farewell, grateful for that necklace hidden in those nefarious pillows, and that gift of a tiny, restless quail egg placed inside your only love letter. My body is a love letter too. Naked, I contemplate myself. I also love these tokens on my body, these limp crevices, which, for one terrifying moment, were yours. Faces of love on the shadow of your mouth.

I am writing you this love letter because I am at peace. You owe me nothing, only the tremendous happiness of having been able to invent you, and fantasize about those rendezvous that never were, mesmerized by the voice on the telephone, and those love letters which will never be read out loud, because I never received them. And now, I am sending you this letter. And my hand reaches up near yours to help you read it, so my breath will help you penetrate this velvet evening like a mad, indomitable heart. Like a furious and sublime verse. Like the most infinite love, wrapped in the paper of invisible orange blossoms.

THE BOTTLE

I have been thrust in this transparent, aromatic, bottle of water for twenty five years now. I am able to let my hair fall free as it tangles itself with the evening seaweed and the malefic noise of the ocean in the shadows. It was I who decided to enter this glassy space where no one dares to look at me. But I can see everything from the safety of this hiding place which in no way belongs to my children or my husband. When I disappeared, they went to look for me at the shoe store, then the post office. That s why I write letters madly without any addresses or addressees. But I write them just the same. For five days they searched for me. They put two notices in the local newspaper, but, they forgot about me.

I saw them return happily from their daily tasks to sell my furniture, the mirrors, and my see-through underwear. I watched as they invited the rabbi and the priest to say that I was a generous, hospitable woman. And I would laugh because I didn t like to look at them. I was tired of having them ask me to do things; cutting their bangs, sewing their shoes, cooking hot dogs, being told to speak or not to speak, going to pick them up, fixing their ties, the chairs, percale skirts... I used to go to bed exhausted, like a petrified prune. And that s what they call the joy of motherhood.

For a long time I dreamed of being invisible, of scaring them in the bath tub and drowning them. But I couldn t do it. My pacifist religion wouldn t allow me to do it until I got the idea about the bottle, and here I am. My husband married a woman as strange as I am. She dusts the furniture for him, straightens the sheets, irons his shirts and his penis, and he touches her as if she were his cellular phone. I smile, and don t even cry, or should I say I cry a lot less, because there is no room in this bottle for tears. I have enough space for my heart to beat and to be content. To be visible, or invisible. The water makes me happy. It relaxes me and makes my face longer. My hair has turned into seaweed. I am dead or alive. Perhaps. To rest at long last. True happiness.

A RECENT NAKEDNESS

This desire, like a tickle of invisible aromas, penetrates the golden crevices of my skin. Desire is what I long for, and I place myself on top of him the way one makes love over a lawn of yellow leaves. I desire the crazed magnitude of winged carpets exploring me in my recent nakedness. It is the body I desire, wreaking vengeance upon clothing, descending into the tranquility of glistening sheets, like the shrouds of the good life.

Tickling, climbing, desire up my knees, making me perspire from joy and fright. This is the desire of longing to be with all of them and none of them; of making love in a convent, in a desert tent, or at the bottom of the ocean, with long seaweed hair for a bed. It is the desire of never wanting men who wear silk socks.

Ever since I turned fifty, I haven t been a woman in my fifties. I am a delicious woman. I contemplate myself with each of my imperfections: my breasts gravitating close to the middle of the sky, my crooked legs, my varicose veins like rivers, my ash white hair, and I am happy. At last, I like myself, and I like men of all ages, sizes, and nationalities. How beautiful it would be to love in Chinese, Bengali, or Sudanese. How beautiful to have a court of people from foreign lands to write of love s fiestas in rare tongues.

Ever since I began to ask myself about desire, I always wear perfume and saturate myself with birds and bonfires. I am a lover of luxuriant desire, and all I ever want to do is remember- remember your breath, and your legs split apart in the vastness. I wish to be a crescent for your voice, forever remembering desire, like the snow, invincible in its wordlessness.

LIFE INSIDE OF LOVE

Let me gaze at you in this serene and treacherous nakedness. Be still as if time and the cloak of the evening were to unravel you. Let me look at you in this place of emptiness so I can call out to you. Don t move. Give me the gift of your navel and the soft texture of your thighs tangled within your arms. Let me create you with my eyes so your face will always be with me. Then I will sense the rapture of imagining you all naked- as if you were deep inside the water, deep inside an island, or deep inside my body-trembling between the light, the veil of the afternoon, and the breath of a kiss. Let me gaze at you.

TICKLE OF LOVE

As soon as it dawns, I can sense the tremblings all over my body, as if my skin were sliding on top of things. Then I feel an extraordinary, tremendous urge to think about love, to make love in church doorways wearing my star of David so that no one will have a doubt about the fact that Jewish women are not decapitated monsters. I get deep, penetrating chills and want to dig inside myself as if that thing called desire could spring up from the bottom of my body. But it's impossible to explain that thing about desire, that tickling sensation between my legs, on the tips of my fingers, in the openings of my nose and mouth. I can't touch it or describe it. I can only say, for instance, that while traveling on an airplane, I would be delighted to undress the pilot, open the exit window, and make love to him out in the open clouds.

I like men in uniforms but not men in the military. I am referring to waiters, plumbers, gardeners, mailmen, dentists and maybe a few doctors. There is no trade union as far as sex is concerned. Everything is a burning possibility. I don't care whether they're fat or thin, bald or boring, or have little golden feet. What is important is having the fantasy, the journey of desire. To walk down the street and imagine that when I cross at the corner someone will take me away to a room filled with burnt red autumn leaves. He will undress me at the center of a radiant, late afternoon light. He will tell me that for seven years he has been thinking about me and my body, my hands, my shoulders. He will tell me not to hurry because we have all afternoon to caress each other.

Sometimes I imagine I am not in New York, or Boston, or any city of exiles. I imagine I am in my city, Santiago, Chile, next to the Andes mountains. And I dream that at last we have buried all of the dead, and the tortured people can go outside and get drunk, or have a cup of coffee with a little slice of toast. I dream about all of these things, but shudder to think of desire, of someone's breath, or sex, as a mantle to cure death, which is forever inopportune.

Of all the men I have loved, I still remember their little aromas and the way they bent their knees after love. I still keep tiny strands of their hair, the tissues moistened in alcohol and a bit of their semen. I am sixty years old, and I still think about the birds that used to go through our room, and how you wanted to open the window to placate the mists and tender bonfires of love. Silently, I told you no, to let the birds and the bonfires, the winter with its white horses, pass through our room.

I asked everything of you in silence, a wicked and beloved silence, one that is the sickness of love. At last, after seven years, you dared to travel a path of my sex that did not belong to the evening. And it was the blue color of the birds that perch upon your shoulders. After seven years you insisted there was no need for haste because time and celebration, spring and the gazes were all with us. And I no longer got undressed, crazy as moonshine or darkened like a woman who is finally desired, as if God had intervened in the sacred practice of love. Now this time, take all of your clothes off.

You look like a tree full of shadows and lights. You have the body of a sleeping boy. You seem to be a misplaced and solitary traveler when you play with the brittle moment of my ear.

The room is going around. It is white, reddish, and ocher. I ask you to open the windows so I can look at you. And you laugh. I ask you to tell me about the kites, the time you worked at the greenhouse, and I am sure that no one will be capable of coming in to shave our heads, disguising our sick or healthy desire; that no one will be capable of taking this life away from us, the life that is born when you kiss me, when you caress my bent and hidden thigh. And I know that not even the walls of these rooms will be able to tell this story, because this is a love like the things of winter: ragged, humble and generous. More than anything, it is a love of two foreigners inside the body of one ambiguous country.

When the moment of death comes, I know that you and I will be on the thresholds of that room. The horsemen of the Apocalypse will give us permission to love each other one last time. I will repeat your name as if it were a cherished address, so as not to lose you, so I can have you, and keep you close to the entrance of my sex. But now, time will not matter. God waits for the merciful and the good, and this time we will be together without the urgency that you must be on your way, or that your wife is calling, or you can't sell your furniture, your books, or your love letters. Or you can't forgive yourself because you loved me so cautiously and so madly.

When it is time to die, desire is like a tilting lamp that

helps us feel comfortable, and our body covers us with glowing shrouds.

I am eighty years old and I am an exquisite old lady. Naked at the time of rest, I have returned to adolescence. Someone has closed my eyelids. Then, I tremble like never before. I see your mouth, every mouth; I see my sex, open and moist; I see backs, the evening, and my healthy body that was never wounded. And now, at death, I feel that same tickling sensation, that crazy urge to make love and think about desire all through the blessed day. And luckily, I have found a lot of dead men who also have time for that delicious, invisible coitus called desire, called the tickle of love.

BOUGAINVILLAEA INSOMNIA CHAPTER VI

DREAMER OF FISHES

Of all the stories, her favorite was the one about the mermaids, those most venerable and shimmering inhabitants of the sea. Thinking about them with that air of women held captive, their legs wrapped in violet scales, gave her so much pleasure that she was able to keep awake for seven or even fourteen nights in a row. This she did in step with the sweetness of a song she sang to herself in order to stay awake forever and imagine the mermaids.

My mother, Frida Eugenia, suffered from fabricated insomnia. In other words, she wanted to see so many things at night that she was unable to see during the day, that she decided not to sleep. That way she could take pleasure in the scenes she had collected from her journeys and moments of ecstasy. And like Ulysses, my mother used to cover her ears during the day so she wouldn t have to listen to the neighbor s chatter, injure her children s sweetness, or be forced to partake of the daily rituals. Then, at night, she was free to let in every tide and earthquake- and that happiness- like an evening of gossamer cloaks and ancient landscapes of loves and the seas.

My mother was always naked when she slept, and she never wore gold chains or even her greenish silver ring. She used to say a body needed solitude to remember, that memory became unleashed when glistening skin looked back at itself. It was easier for her not to surrender to sleep because misfortune had taught her that joy does not come in any particular shape (not even in the shape of wooden boards), as if joy itself were a matter of random noonday dreams.

My mother used to lie awake in her bed. Moreover, she was a euphoric sleepwalker. In order to keep herself awake during the day she would write about her dreams. Often, she would choose a forest of algae and imagine the mermaids gleaming skin flowing through a sargasso sea, or verdant lettuce plants shedding their leaves like a chloroform dream.

The color green filled her with great elation. She used to say that it was possible to stay awake and alert in among the rich thickness of the forest s liquid glances.

On one of her sleepless nights, she told me she was dreaming about the old Lisboa Amalfi neighborhood. She was soaring in a frenzy. And inside decrepit passageways she could hear melodious voices stalking her body, luring her to dance. On another evening, she swore she had seen the coffins of the dead fly down a hill and go wild before the passage of death. And right at this moment, she is telling me she used to dream of being a Bolero dancer.

When I became infected with the desire for insomnia, sometimes I drew closer to her and looked at her smooth, clear, tongue that glowed when it stammered, because when my mother was unable to sleep, she began to talk and recite, sing and pray, and out of her mouth came both alien and familiar words. It was so deliciously beautiful to watch her sleep as she traveled across the feats of the day, because her mouth was like a carnival all lit up.

And in between her teeth, I could see that blazing froth of joy.

PINE TREES

She liked the house because it was close to the sea. In truth, it was deep inside a fantastical woods and from behind a hill the sea looked like a green mirage. In the afternoon she liked to go to the edge of the forest, stretch out her hand and watch the rhythm of the bandurrias or fireflies making phosphorescent celebrations in between her bones.

On evenings of fever and rage, when the city glowed as if blinded by an unassuming air of terror, she would walk towards her house, intoxicated, crossing uninhabited streets and plazas brimming with human life. When she reached the great door, the pine trees would light up and bow at her arrival. Then, as the lights of the evening and the quivering flame were beginning to grow brighter, she would dream for hours, lying with her eyes bandaged, devising the ideal being.

He had huge hands to caress her with, hands to split her open as he went close to her barefoot body. The seagulls arrived, and every landscape held itself inside her like the calm breath of an ocean in love. He told her she had hair like Marilyn Monroe. He told her that ever since she was a child and had come to that same house of beach aromas when the sand had made her hair even more copper, he had desired her, had wanted to make her stand still and tangle her hair with the pine trees, the leaves, and all the forest's belongings, there, inside that distant house by the sea.

When they went to look for her they arrived at the house on a day when there were no rains or evil omens. She was thinking of Marilyn Monroe and the furrow of death. She wore a white nightgown and smelled of moss and seaweeds. They took her away and the house was left empty. But the ancient timbers didn't rot, the bulwark stood its ground, and the ocean never really got too close.

When she returned to her country with her soul boarded up and the profile of her body wounded upon her gaze, her only wish was to reach the house. And she went in the winter when the fog seeps in all over and the whispers of darkness crackle. And there was the house, and the sheets all spread out with the outline of a body that loves. It was still there, with the old blankets from the south and the clay pots collected from journeys lost. When the pine trees saw her pass by they bowed as if they had been waiting for her. He told her she still had hair like Marilyn Monroe and said her face was the beginning of summer. Then he suggested they go inside the house where no one would see them and they could surround themselves in the mists.

THE TOWER

The hotel was pointed and very, very green. Its oval walls permeated the contour of the hill, the pasture lands, and the sea glimmering in the distance like a lone and faithful watchman. The little girl liked the hotel, which almost seemed enclosed by the deepest part of the forest, filled with pasture aromas and that fleeting odor of time.

The little girl used to travel with her mother and father around the city's narrow periphery. And despite the fact that the city had been formed at the absolute bottom of the sea, it looked like one of those cities without water.

For years, as in the seasons of contentment and custom, the little girl knew that every Sunday she would carry with her the glances she had saved in order to be able to climb with her imaginary friend to the top of the highest tower of the hotel, invisible in between the masked sea and the soothing, verdant sweat of New Zealand meadows.

When she was an adolescent she used to leave the house in a hurry and almost seem perplexed. Then, she would run until she reached the doors of the hotel, as if inside that rocky and peculiar building, forgotten souls were waiting for her. When she turned thirteen, the first relatives of that quiet family began to die off. At home, they covered up the mirrors and kept a silent vigil filled with shadows and bitter voices. And it was at that time, because they feared for the girl immersed by the vapors of death, that they sent her away to the hotel of her dreams and her flights.

They told her to stay in the room near the cupola until the smell of death had navigated through the oceans of the south and penetrated the Tasmanian sea. She accepted with the easiness of a woman familiar with the transformations of destiny. She then entered the hotel to fill herself with the odor of emptiness from the luxuriant wood that lived inside those uninhabited spaces. And from the cupola of the bell tower she could watch the passage of the wind and the tricks of the sea.

For two days the girl lived happily in that hotel, cast within the plains. The air of death did not go near her. On the contrary, joy consisted of looking at delicate boats, quicksand, and the army of birds and the albatross that came to the windows near the fringes of the skies.

More than anything, the girl hoped for the death of her relatives so she could return to the hotel and take a rest from the heavy silence of her parents' ordeal; harvesting the dead and putting them away in the back rooms of horror.

For a period of three summers, the girl's family began to die. At times, in the middle of insanity and abandon, she would think that the rituals of death were her fault. But the simple fact of spending an evening in a room at the hotel made her crazy with joy.

During adolescence she became aware of the death of

three generations. She knew of the bodies' disappearance into the sea, and their ashes. But nothing moved her. Her only wish was to return to the bell tower, stretch out on the blue blanket, plunge herself into the fiesta of the fireflies, and celebrate once more the arrival of bodies and seaweed from behind the ocean swell.

Although she still looked fresh and her face had not retained the harsh passage of time, the girl reached old age. On moon days it was possible to see the clarity, the hidden drops of water on her doll-like eyelids. However, in the face of her own death, or the death of others, she remained untouched. In spite of everything, the hotel was always an uninhabited space where she could still dream of climbing way to the top and look out at the sparkling, bewildered sea behind the portals of the afternoon.

The day of her death came quickly and unexpectedly. This time no one deposited her anonymously and dazed behind the doors of that hotel with its blue awnings and blue windows looking like a desert of water. This time, no one came to the door to tell her she could return home. She had buried all of them and was happy in the days of her death because she celebrated birthdays of love and sweet contentment.

On the day of her death, she was already at the hotel resting on a pillow of coarse rocks. She was there, filled with glances and words. Death awaited her in that empty room with the silent bodies of loved ones and alphabets with their names, and she became a cloak of joy. It was only then that her face was able to harden with the indentations of old age. At last, she would no longer bury the others. At last, she and the hotel became one fiesta of silent bodies.

POSTCARDS

Marisol Cifuentes wasn't a woman accustomed to the accumulation of ceremonial objects or sacred memory. On the contrary, when they found her in that cabin within the temperate ripple of the forest, we realized that as time went on, she had gotten rid of her furniture, the walls had upheld the true secret of emptiness, and her room still carried the aroma of a moist, white sheet. What they did find in that dead woman's dislocated home were several postcards which Marisol Cifuentes kept in a motheaten book of imaginary addresses.

One of the postcards revealed the lights of Paris reflecting on a fountain. It was clear from the handwriting on the card that it belonged to someone who had loved her and remembered her as if he were traveling close to her gaze all through the most beautiful and extraordinary cities.

It was a well-known fact that the woman in question had been born in that city without a sea. Mired in the dusty jungle and the inharmonious obsession of loneliness, she had made her cabin where other ancestors had built the house where Marisol Cifuentes now lay sleeping in death.

The postcards had been preserved intact, you might even say, flawlessly, right in the midst of that explosive poverty and the smell of a dead woman climbing up the void. The card with a bridge on it from the city of Bruges, was the most conspicuous one because it suggested a gentle invitation. There were words like "come" and "cross it." And on the side in tiny handwriting the minuscule word "come."

The attempt to locate the sender of these missives in order to let that someone know of Marisol Cifuentes' slow death in the middle of the evening's quiet fire holding in her arm those five recollected postcards, was all in vain.

The few neighbors who went to the place of her death seemed surprised to find that Marisol Cifuentes was still pretty, despite her loneliness. From among the sheets there appeared an old worn-out address book where Marisol had collected the names of beings who have yet to enter the sphere of reality. They also seemed to be the titles of certain paintings, the names of works of art, or former movie stars like John Nelson and Eddy and Janet McDonald. But not a single name gave a clue as to the identity of that traveler who embarked on a journey of each city with the image of Marisol's face, talking to her in museums, calling her to mind at each bridge, comparing her to the lights of Paris, promising her secrets, perhaps.

MISTS

With gargantuan jaws, the insects gouge the fog that seeps through the forest thickness, dark and radiant. The silence is frightening from so much peace. Only in that dark space of time did the small girl wake up, thirsty with rage, seeking even further those last shreds of darkness. The servants used to remain at her side without speaking, as if the essence of a shadow had covered their etched and weatherbeaten faces.

The servants were there, keeping watch over the child's sleep, fanning her with the leaves of a bewitched palm tree. When the sun crackled, they cut the leaves from the highest and brightest palm trees so the child's awakening would be airy and transparent.

Like statues held prisoner before an incarnate destiny, the servants would fan the child for hours on end with deliberate and agitated movements. Not even the slightest gesture of anger could be perceived in them, only a resignation which dates back thousands of years. The girl would wake up making faces, and she laughed with a mixture of modesty and perverse pleasure. The silent ladies would begin to bathe her with coconut elixir and lavender from Saint Remy, which used to arrive on the coasts in ships carrying clandestine slaves.

Morning activities were taken up dressing the girl, combing her long and listless locks, perfuming her with lavender. Then they would carry her to the breakfast room where she drank fresh goat's milk and ate bread just out of the oven seated at a rectangular table all by herself. Alone, while the servants continued to fan her with huge palm leaves, the girl continued to live in the same fashion, a little anxious and a little frightened. There she was in that remote place in a house inhabited by servants and a girl who couldn't even find her breath in the mirror because her legs were growing thin from being served so much. On sunny days when she had her period, they would keep her in a languid state, resting in the open air of that static and ancient summer. They used to think that the heat and the mists would dry up her blood or fill her, perhaps, with a sweetness like the nectar of those unmentionable tropical places.

Late in the evening, they would carry her inside, disfigured now from so much rest. There, they continued to fan her until the light seeped in and the night appeared like a great mouth unable to utter even the sounds of the wind, the elves, or the witches who used to wander in search of the vulnerable souls of the maids.

The maids stayed with her for more than twenty years and watched her fall apart from too many ailments. They saw her body swell with mischievous fruits and her hands turn into maimed fragments. Her fingers were calcified and green from being fanned so often with those nefarious palm leaves. So they finally decided to leave her because their hour of death had also come.

Way before the dawn. Before they prepared the palm leaf fans and the elixir of coconut and lavender, they retreated, naked and all alone beneath the insolent and wounded sun of the Caribbean sea. The girl woke up alone and asphyxiated by the languor of sleep. When she didn't see the servants, she wandered down a path. Then she looked for them behind the decaying furniture. She went to their rooms beyond the gates. She shouted out in rage and terror. When she knew she was no longer with them, she didn't even know how to recognize herself in the mirror. Then, weakened from lack of exercise, she too walked toward the luxuriant green density of the forests and the void, toward the moisture of the fog and the crickets.

BOUGAINVILLAEA INSOMNIA

Of all the seasons, my mother chose the summer to put her dreams and fantasies in order. She used to say that on those listless winter afternoons, inside a huge notebook filled with recipes and shopping lists, she kept written the things she wanted to remember: celebrations of insomnia, countries to visit. My mother was very wise because she had several notebooks where she wrote down her wishes. Once, she wrote: visit the Galápagos Islands, return to the cave of the first albatross, sleep among the conifers, reach the Tasmanian Sea by umbrella.

In the light of summer, when the day and a glance grow longer, she would lay bare the passage of her dreams, and take delight in the adoring pleasure of her everlasting wakefulness.

My mother is still full of dreams. Her body is clothed in ropes and shrouds which help her to stay alive, even though she is more than a hundred years old. Her mouth won t close because of her overpowering wish to live forever, to lick the very last recesses of her tears, and to feel the palpitation of desire. She has gathered so many illusions that she is unable to die. Do not misjudge her. You see, she did not choose insomnia. It was just that her astonished look didn t want to miss anything because it had the flavor of an implacable fantasy, and even the crazy longing to taste the bougainvilleas. . . .

WITCHES

In the evening when darkness climbs on the hidden periphery of wood. When the soul meanders half-drowsy and half-restless, there, on the last edge of darkest darkness, I approach the leaves that set themselves aflame with just a look, and wait for the coming of the witches. I know they appear unseen and long for someone to wait for them the way one waits for love or the eternal passage of events. I look out onto the terrace. The village has no sea, but I can imagine its long weeds like the manes of dead women. Then I prepare to wait for them because they arrive at the most unexpected times without ever being inopportune.

One need not look at witches in order to love them because they are like secrets of the soul. Aloof and intimate they draw near leaving furrows and marks on the faces they touch. They are soft and distant. They are made of water and sugar.

Witches love the summer because they keep luxuriant bunches of grapes between their legs. And contrary to what is believed, they like to play in the light when the pale magic of blossoms and hollyhocks covers the enormous ocean sky. Then they appear like fireflies or translucent butterflies evoking the aromatic herbs of late, green afternoons. The boldest witches wink their eyes and a spell is carved on a gaze of silk.

Of all the witches, the ones I like most wear green vestments and prepare potions inside the leafy exuberance of tree trunks. I love the ones who repeat words full of bliss as if they were a set of golden beads. I like to see them squatting and naked, without that perverse, gray, wardrobe we mortals use. They are there in the middle of the woods, in the middle of fear and enchantment. They are right there, in those secret hiding places, like an everlasting and unexplainable fragrance.

I love witches when they go to parties dressed in red velvet. They sit with their legs half-open and only wise men can look at the darkening light of their pubis where their sex begins and desire becomes entangled. Those witches in red velvet light up with passion and drink happily with blushed faces. They are herbalists brimming with flowers. They are prudent and always honest and mischievous.

In the evening when the afternoon starts to mingle with the first wounds of darkness, all of the children wait for the witches to come. They tremble with joy to think of the winged witches perching warmly on the blankets of their dreams. I too wait for them with a fear that is only felt when one loves happiness. They are approaching now. I can hear them like the trains of a lost city. They enter my bed. They are the very root and secret of dreams. They intuit my geography, straighten out my covers, and take off their clothes. The red velvet becomes a gigantic blanket of fire. I talk with them but I do not cross the thresholds of their spells. I am merely with them. I ask them for orange blossoms, gardenias, and herbs for loving or curing envy. But they are preparing a banquet for me. There are no goats or hungry cats, only sunflowers, strawberries, and warm wines, like the fires of true love. With them beside me, I devour life. I remove all of my clothing so I can hear them better. I adore them with their fantastical capes, wary steps, and shy look. Every afternoon I sit down to wait for them. Among the late day leaves I build a blue bonfire from my eyes. And they appear before the mirrors, the sunrise, the beginning of time, and you.

WINE

I

Wine through seasons lost. Wine through every insomnia. They drink in the peace of abandonment and know that the union inside the fullness of their lover's body was deprivation. They drink behind a devoured fog of remoteness to cover up their sorrows because intoxication is a hidden caress. In barren lands the woman drinks. Dejected ingrate, she draws tiny furrows with her mouth, shattered like the final holy place of all her insanities.

II

She drinks so she will be able to talk about everything. She approaches emptiness through the silences of bittersweet wine like crippled songs and what inhabits the secret memory of things. All through the evening we drank at the house in the stupor of desire. At the beach we drank blissfully, consumed by a time of ashes. And they are euphoric and content as long as the illusory substance ripples over their bodies. They drink the desecration of happiness and stolen time. They drink in haste and enraged, in search of high places.

III

I used to drink alone as if lying in wait. Drink took me closer to the exact roundness of circumstance. I could be heroic, avoid silence and confuse drunkenness with desire. For many years, for more than twenty, I drank alone in the late afternoon until I reached the veritable depths of the night. In wine I found no comfort or company for this loneliness which is like a blemish on my skin. Alcohol brought me nearer to insanity and the regions of pain and beauty. With it I invented words. I was closer to books and conversations. But I drank only as far as happiness and the death of that happiness. And I always drank in pain and isolation, like a woman all alone.

ABOUT THE AUTHOR

MARJORIE AGOSIN, noted poet and human rights activitist, is professor of Spanish Literature at Welesley College. She is the recipient of many awards both in Latin America and the United States, including most recently the Letras de Oro Prize (1995) and the Latino Literature Prize (1995). She is the author of numerous books of poetry, short stories and criticism, and editor of many important anthologies of Latin American women writers. Women in Disguise her her second book of short stories to appear in English.